QWERTY MURDERS

Pippa Parker Mysteries: 5

Liz Hedgecock

WHITE
RHINO
BOOKS

For Stephen,
who would always come with me
to the library

CHAPTER 1

Pippa Parker stifled a rude word as the second alarm, the one labelled *Go NOW*, shrilled on her phone. 'All right, all right, I'm coming,' she muttered as she saved the document she was working on and closed her laptop. For today was Tuesday, and on a Tuesday, for reasons she had never fathomed, her mother-in-law Sheila couldn't possibly mind Ruby after three o'clock.

Pippa slipped her shoes on and grabbed her keys. Was it worth getting the car out? The traffic crawling past the end of the cul-de-sac said *Fat chance*. She set off at a brisk walk in the direction of Sheila's house, avoiding the wet leaves on the pavement. *Please be in a good mood,* she thought, mentally crossing her fingers.

Sheila's wary expression lightened at the sight of Pippa, whose heart sank. 'Oh hello dear. Gosh, is it that time already? Ruby, Mummy's here!'

The only answer was the faint noise of the television, which sounded as if it was broadcasting the sort of cartoon which Sheila normally termed a brain-rotter.

Sheila tried again. 'Ruby!'

'I don't want to!' came the reply. On other days Pippa might have been proud that her almost-two-year-old could speak in complete sentences. However, today was not one of those days.

'I'll fetch her,' she said, stepping over the threshold and bracing herself.

Ruby was ensconced in a nest of cushions on the sofa, a packet of crisps in her hand, and eyes glued to the television. 'Come on, trouble,' said Pippa, unpacking Ruby from her cushion fort. 'Time to fetch Freddie.' Her eyes narrowed. 'You weren't wearing that when I dropped you off.' Ruby was resplendent in a floaty pink dress with wings, tiara and wand.

'Dress-up,' said Ruby, dismissively, in an *I-woke-up-like-this* sort of way.

'Whatever,' Pippa replied, feeling sulky. 'Now if you could magic us to school so that we're *not* late —'

Ruby let out a teenage sigh and put her arms up to be lifted off the sofa, clinging to her half-empty packet of crisps.

'Thanks, Sheila,' said Pippa, wedging Ruby against her and making for the door. 'Must dash. Oh, where are Ruby's shoes?'

Sheila bent, with an effort, and handed Pippa the sparkly plimsolls which Ruby had been wearing that morning.

'No!' said Ruby, shaking her head emphatically.

'What, so you're going to walk through the village

2

barefoot?' Pippa replied, fitting one shoe onto Ruby's dangling foot.

Ruby kicked it off. '*No!* Fairy shoes!'

Pippa gritted her teeth and dipped for the shoe. Ruby shrieked and her little fingers dug into Pippa's arm.

'Good luck,' said Sheila, opening the door.

'Where the car?' wailed Ruby, flinging an arm at the vast inhospitable desert which was her home, Much Gadding.

'At home,' snapped Pippa. 'Where I wish I was right now. Bye, Sheila. Enjoy the peace and quiet.'

'I shall,' said Sheila, grinning. 'I feel a nice cup of tea coming on.'

Pippa made an inarticulate noise and started down the path.

It wasn't far to Freddie's school, but Pippa's wriggly, constantly-shifting burden slowed her considerably. Ahead she could see other parents with their toddlers and preschoolers, all walking nicely, holding hands and *wearing shoes*. 'See those children behaving themselves, Ruby?' she said, resettling Ruby on her hip. 'That's what you should be doing.'

'That's lame,' said Ruby, smugly.

'Where on earth did you learn that?' asked Pippa, but Ruby turned her tiaraed head away.

And now the big boys and girls were walking out of the school gates and home. Pippa increased her pace and Ruby yelped, holding her tiara on with one hand. Several parents Pippa recognised from Freddie's class nodded to her with sympathetic smiles as they led their children off the premises.

Miss Darcy, Freddie's teacher even though she looked as if she had escaped from an A-level course, was standing at the door to the reception classroom, holding Freddie's hand. 'Not *again,* Mummy,' he said reproachfully.

'Sorry, Freddie,' Pippa said, holding her hand out to him. 'Sorry, Miss Darcy. Her Majesty here wasn't in the mood for walking. Or shoes.'

Ruby wiggled her feet and stared at Miss Darcy, who appeared rather embarrassed. 'I like your rainbow,' she said.

'Oh, um, thank you,' said Miss Darcy, putting a hand to her long brown hair, where, sure enough, was a glittery rainbow clip.

'Can I have it?' asked Ruby, stretching out a hand.

'No you can't,' said Pippa. 'We'll try to be on time tomorrow, Miss Darcy. Well, we try every day, but somehow we don't ever manage it. Come along, Freddie.'

'Goodbye, Miss Darcy,' said Freddie, ever so nicely, and waved goodbye as Pippa shepherded him down the path. Miss Darcy waved back. 'Can we go to the tearoom?'

'Nope,' said Pippa, 'my purse is at home.'

'Ohhhhhh,' wailed Freddie. 'But I'm *hungry.*'

Pippa sneaked a glance as they turned the corner. Yes, Miss Darcy was still there, had almost certainly heard, and probably thought she was the worst mother in the world. 'You're always hungry. Will a chocolate biscuit and milk when you get home do?'

'S'pose,' said Freddie. But he said it with a grin on his face, and his getting-bigger-but-still-little hand squeezed

4

hers.

***

Pippa's phone buzzed in her jeans pocket several times on the way home, but there was no chance of checking her messages; not with Ruby on her hip and Freddie chattering about his day. 'An' we did big maths, Mummy, and Miss Darcy read us *The Gruffalo*, an' then we did paintings and Miss Darcy said mine was super-scary.'

'Excellent,' said Pippa.

'And I had spaghetti bonolese for lunch —'

'I can tell,' said Pippa, eyeing Freddie's polo shirt, where splotches of red sauce competed with splats of brown and green and orange paint. Sometimes she wondered if the school had shares in a washing-powder company.

'And chocolate sponge and custard for pudding.'

Freddie paused for breath and Pippa dived in. 'All that, and you're still hungry?'

'We did dodgeball this afternoon.' Freddie closed his mouth with the satisfied look of a boy who has delivered a killer argument.

'Ahhhh.' Pippa fished for her keys and the phone buzzed again.

'Can I watch *MegaMoose* please?'

Pippa almost dropped her keys as well as her jaw. 'Not *SuperMouse?*'

Freddie shrugged and made a noise which could have been 'meh'. 'Jake says *MegaMoose* is awesomer. He has secret things in his antlers!'

'Wow.' Pippa got the door open and thankfully set

5

Ruby down on the hall floor. 'Is it on a channel we have?'

'I'll go see,' said Freddie, and scampered into the lounge. Ruby pointed her wand at his retreating back, but thankfully nothing happened.

'Kettle *on*,' Pippa muttered to herself. She poured two beakers of milk for the children, put two small chocolate biscuits each on two plastic plates, and reached into the cupboard for her *Buffy the Vampire Slayer* mug.

Buzzzz.

'Oh come off it,' said Pippa, and breathed in to retrieve her phone. The screen showed several messages, in reverse order of their arrival.

Lila: *I think flamingoes would be ace but would Lady H mind?*

Simon: *Do we need wine for tonight?*

Lila: *Parrots or flamingoes, what do you think?*

Serendipity: *Could you call me, Pippa. Something's happened.*

Lila: *I found a shop on eBay that does grass skirts and flower garlands.*

Lady H: *Do I need to pay the application fee first? Please advise.*

Jeff: *Help, Lila's gone mad. She wants our wedding dress code to include grass skirts?!?!?*

Lady H: *The venue application form came in the post at lunchtime. Would you be able to pop in tomorrow and help me with it?*

Pippa put the phone on the worktop, closed her eyes,

and took a few deep breaths.

'*MegaMoose* is on the KidzFun channel!'

Pippa's eyes jolted open. Freddie appeared pleased. 'Can I please can I?'

'OK.' Pippa handed him a beaker and a plate. 'Is Ruby watching with you?' *Please say yes*.

Freddie nodded, and Pippa took Ruby's snack through to the lounge, where Ruby was curled up in the armchair, both wings on the same side and her tiara crooked in her dark curls. 'Wouldn't you be more comfortable without the wings?' said Pippa.

Ruby shot her a scornful glance, then saw the biscuits. 'Thank you Mummy,' she said, with an angelic smile.

'Cupboard love,' said Pippa, and retreated to the kitchen. While the kettle boiled she got her thumbs busy:

Lila: *I suspect the grass skirts would be a bigger problem than the flamingoes*

Jeff: *I'll try and talk her down*

Simon: *YES red please*

Lady H: *Yes I can and no idea, will look tomorrow*

Life seemed to have become very busy all of a sudden. Pippa had thought she was busy before, but Lady Higginbotham had taken everything up a notch. The Much Gadding proms at Higginbotham Hall had financed the renovation of two shacks into respectable holiday cabins; Pippa managed the bookings. These financed further repairs on the Hall, which was now watertight, damp-free, and being decorated room by room.

Lady Higginbotham's latest wheeze was to apply for a wedding licence for the Hall. Pippa wondered if Jeff's proposal to Lila at the first prom concert had put the idea into her head. If so, she only had herself to blame, but the potential stream of weddings made Pippa feel dizzy. Especially as Lila had hired her as wedding planner, and had her heart set on something different every week. So far Pippa had a guest list, and a date, and Higginbotham Hall as the wedding venue. Everything else was up in the air. Including whether the Hall would have its licence by the big day.

Pippa sighed, drowned her teabag in boiling water, and chased it round the mug with a spoon. By comparison, Serendipity's events were a doddle. Even the recent photo shoot for her first book had gone like clockwork, since Serendipity's formidable organisation coupled with a week of beautiful weather had made everything a piece of her perfectly-baked rainbow cake (page 49). When the book was close to launch there would be festival bookings and press releases and media work; but until then —

I wonder what Serendipity wants, thought Pippa. She made her tea, then stuck her head into the lounge, where both children were gazing at a moose with a satellite dish on one antler and a spork on the other. 'I'm making a phone call, kids, I'll be in the dining room.'

Both nodded without turning their heads.

Pippa reopened her laptop and found Serendipity's bookings spreadsheet. Everything seemed to be in hand; in fact things were quietening down after a rush of summer fairs. She rang Serendipity's number, and waited.

Serendipity picked up on the second ring. 'Oh Pippa, thank you so much for calling me. It's — oh, it's just awful, and I don't know what to do.'

'Are you all right?' Pippa asked automatically, even though Serendipity sounded far from all right. 'What's happened?'

'Nothing. Yet. But it will. They'll make me, and it'll be awful. Everything I've worked for —'

'Who will make you? Make you do what?'

'I can't do this on the phone,' muttered Serendipity. 'Can I come round?'

Pippa's gaze slid to the wall dividing the dining room from the lounge. 'Course you can. I'll put a film on for the kids.'

'Thanks.' A small sniff. 'It's — You'll probably think it's an opportunity, but believe me, it won't be.' Serendipity already sounded defeated. 'Is ten minutes OK?'

'Sure.'

'See you soon, then.' And the call ended. Pippa drank some tea, then closed the laptop. Whatever Serendipity was upset about, it wasn't her current work. *I could do something if it was*, thought Pippa, feeling helpless. As it was, perhaps a listening ear and a cup of tea was all she could offer.

CHAPTER 2

'A reality show?'

Serendipity cupped her hands round her mug and studied the table. 'Yes. *Keeping Up With The Skeffington-Joneses*. That's the working title.'

'But I thought your parents were dead against anything...' Pippa racked her brain for the right word, 'popular.'

'They were,' said Serendipity, gazing into her mug as if her fortune might appear at the bottom. 'Until the roof fell in at Skeffington Towers.'

'Is that the country house?'

Serendipity nodded. 'They've been told it needs to be completely redone, and as it's listed —'

'Oh dear.'

'And what with putting all four of us through school and university, and the estate, and the house in London, and the one in France, and the horses... In short, there isn't much spare money. Not without selling something.

Apparently one of Daddy's friends came up with the idea. He knows a TV executive, and he put in a word. So here we are.'

'But you don't have to be in it.' Pippa patted Serendipity's hand, which was gripping her mug hard enough to shatter it.

'That's the problem. I do. They won't green-light the show unless I'm in three out of the six planned episodes. With at least ten minutes of screen time. For some reason they think I'll be a draw.' Serendipity's tone was bitter as black coffee. 'Bloody YouTube.'

Pippa wished she hadn't wasted her 'oh dear' on the listed roof. 'So what is the show about, exactly?'

Serendipity sighed. 'My family's posh country life; charity balls and riding to hounds and shooting pheasants. Not that they do all those things regularly, but they will on the show.' She wrinkled her nose. 'Oh, and their disappointing daughter too, probably.'

'I assume you've said no.'

'Of course. But Mummy just said, "We'll see, dear." That means she's got something up her sleeve. She said her publicist would phone me. Which she did, when I was on the way here.'

'What did she say?'

'I don't know, I didn't pick up.' Serendipity gulped a mouthful of coffee, then clanked the mug down. 'Mummy tried to convince me that it didn't matter. "No-one will actually watch it," she said. And when I pointed out that the TV company wouldn't be making the show if no-one was going to watch it, she laughed and said. "No-one *we*

11

know." Oh, and apparently all the rest of the family are looking forward to it. I'm the odd one out.' Another sigh. 'As usual.'

'Well, I'm your publicist as much as anyone is, and your friend, and I say don't do it if you don't want to. And you clearly don't want to, so don't do it.'

Serendipity looked at Pippa from under her eyelashes. 'Does that mean you think I should do it, really?'

'No!' Pippa stopped short of smacking her own forehead. 'What did I just say? Ring the publicist and tell her no. You'll feel better, and the matter will be closed.'

Serendipity said nothing, circling her finger round the rim of her mug. Then, softly, 'I'm worried that if I ring her she'll talk me round.'

'For heaven's sake!' Pippa held out her hand. 'Give me your phone. I'll get the publicist's number, call her, and tell her no for you.'

'Would you?' Serendipity asked, her eyes shining.

'Course I would.' Pippa snapped her fingers. 'Phone.'

Serendipity unlocked her mobile and laid it in Pippa's palm like an offering.

'Right.' Pippa found voicemail and pressed *Play* on the last call, then set it to speakerphone. A warm, confident, smiling voice spoke. A voice which Pippa knew well.

'Oh hello Serendipity, this is Suze Hegarty calling. I've just started working with your family, and we've secured a wonderful media opportunity which I'm sure you'll love to be involved in. As it's getting late I'll try you again in the morning. Bye!'

The message ended. 'So will you phone her now and

tell her no thanks?' asked Serendipity, eagerly.

'Um,' said Pippa. 'I'd better prepare myself first.'

Serendipity's face fell. 'Do you know her?'

'We worked together, she was my chief bridesmaid, and I put one of her ex-clients in jail. So yes, she's a passing acquaintance.' Pippa sighed. 'I'll still phone her. But it won't be quite as easy as I thought.'

***

Pippa waited until the children were fed and in bed before steeling herself to ring Suze. 'Can we open the wine?' she asked Simon.

He raised an eyebrow. 'Bad day at the office?'

'I suspect it's about to be. I need to talk to Suze. About work things.'

Simon sighed. 'I'll fetch the corkscrew.'

'I'll be in the dining room,' said Pippa. 'If I don't survive the call, there's a microwave spaghetti carbonara for one in the fridge.' She sat at the table, opened her notebook, wrote *Call with Suze*, and underlined it.

'Hello Pip!' exclaimed Suze. 'Long time no ring! Hang on a minute —' Clattering and fizzing followed, then a sudden improvement in sound quality. 'There. I was in a lift.'

'Of course you were,' said Pippa. 'Hi, Suze. Are you free to talk?'

'Oh yes. I've got a meeting in ten minutes, but I'm fine till then.'

Pippa glanced at the clock. *7.50.* 'At this time?'

'PR never sleeps, Pip.' Suze laughed. 'What can I do for you?'

'I believe you're working with the Skeffington-Joneses —'

'Good grief, news travels fast!' cried Suze. 'Who told you?'

'Serendipity Jones is a friend of mine —'

'Oh *marvellous*! We can hang out on set!'

'Um, I don't think we can. She doesn't want to do the reality show.'

'Mm.' Silence, which grew. 'Does she know what's involved?' asked Suze, in a decidedly less chipper tone.

'I'm pretty sure her mother said, so yes. And it's a definite no.'

'Serendipity wouldn't have to be in every episode. She could even stand in the background and not speak. Maybe.'

Pippa imagined Serendipity looking mutinous in front of a country house. 'Still no.'

'We could showcase her artwork. Or film her teaching a workshop, or shooting one of her videos. That would be really good publicity.'

Pippa sighed. 'Serendipity wanted me to call you because she was worried you'd talk her round. It's a big no.'

'I could talk to the production team about creative input —'

'*No!*' Simon, entering with a glass of wine, froze momentarily, then recovered and put the glass within reach. 'And that's final.'

Suze sighed. 'This does put me in rather a bind, Pippa. You see, the family need the advance from the show to save their house.'

14

'It's roof repairs. Can't they get a loan?'

'That's a bit harsh,' said Suze, reproachfully.

'They could take out a mortgage, or pawn a Rembrandt, or do a fundraising event. But they shouldn't force their daughter into something she doesn't want to do.'

'No-one's forcing anyone to do anything,' said Suze, in a hurt voice. 'But I do think your client should think it over. Sleep on it. It would be a brilliant opportunity, if handled correctly. I mean, I can see how it would open doors for her, and I could help with that.'

'Serendipity is my friend, Suze. I'll pass on what you've said, but unless she phones and tells you otherwise, it's a no. Bye Suze.' And Pippa ended the call before Suze could slide another word in. She put the phone face-down, slid it away from her, and took a sip of wine.

Simon reappeared. 'That sounded fun. Are you still alive?'

Pippa sipped again. 'Just about. I said no to Suze.'

'Really?' Simon took the glass from her and helped himself.

'Mmm. She wants Serendipity to do a reality show.'

'What, one of the ones with bikinis and snogging?'

'No. Possibly worse. Hanging around with her posh family.'

'Ohhhh.' Simon gave the glass back. 'Well done. She'd hate that.'

'Monty would probably chase the pheasants.' Pippa giggled. 'How was work?'

'Fraught. I need the wine as much as you do.'

'Why, what's up?' Simon didn't seem ruffled. Then

again, he rarely did.

'Oh, nothing particular, just stuff.' He paused. 'Could be another merger. Or possibly a takeover.'

'Oh no, not again —'

'It's all right Pippa, we're doing the taking over. If it happens at all, that is.'

'But you're talking about it.'

'We're good at talking.' Simon grinned. 'Seeing as we've transitioned fully now, and I've been the transition manager, then I'm likely to be quite hands-on if we do go ahead.'

The wine in the glass was diminishing rapidly. 'Will that mean meetings at stupid o'clock in the back of beyond?'

'Stupid o'clock, maybe, but the firm's in Gadcestershire.'

Pippa exhaled, slowly. 'That's good.'

'And at least you're not pregnant and we're not renting and my job isn't at risk this time.'

'No.' A wave of gratitude broke over Pippa. 'Will you get a raise?'

Simon looked guarded. 'It's on the table. Don't go buying yourself Agatha Christie first editions yet.'

Pippa grinned. 'You know me so well.'

Her phone buzzed, and light seeped round its edges. She turned it over to read the message.

Suze: *That was a bit abrupt*

Pippa bit her lip. *Sorry*, she replied.

I thought you were more professional than that.

'What's up?' asked Simon. 'You look like a thundercloud.'

'Suze,' said Pippa. 'That's what's up.'

I'm Serendipity's friend, not her publicist, she texted.

The reply came swiftly. *I can tell.*

Then: *I don't think that you have her best interests at heart. Not career-wise, at any rate.*

Maybe careers aren't everything, Pippa shot back.

Mmm. Anyway, must get back to my meeting. It's been fun. Ciao for now x

Then a photo flashed up of the London skyline, clearly taken from somewhere expensive, exclusive, and high up.

'Nice,' said Simon. 'What does that mean?'

Pippa's phone clacked onto the table. 'That means this isn't over.'

'Oh dear,' said Simon. 'I'll get that carbonara for one out. Think I might be needing it.' Pippa frowned at him. 'Only kidding. But I will fetch the wine.'

CHAPTER 3

'Wanna be a fairy!' wailed Ruby.

'Not today,' said Pippa, putting Ruby's arm into her sleeve. 'Today you will be a little girl having fun at nursery.'

Ruby stuck out her bottom lip and folded her arms.

'Mummy!' called Freddie. 'I need a squeezy bottle! We're making rockets today and Miss Darcy said we had to bring one!'

Pippa gritted her teeth. 'Information which would have been useful *yesterday*, Freddie.' She ran downstairs and inspected the washing-up liquid bottle, which was mercifully almost empty. 'Get a cup, Freddie, please.' She squeezed as much of the contents into the cup as she could, rinsed the bottle with water, and handed it to Freddie. 'There. Crisis averted.'

'Yayyy!' cried Freddie, and ran towards the front door squeezing the bottle. Bubbles cascaded into the air.

'Ruby!' called Pippa. 'Time to go!'

Ruby came downstairs, holding on tight to the banister, putting each foot precisely on the step, and pausing between each. 'Today, if you don't mind,' said Pippa, lifting her down the last few steps.

The nursery, also known as the money pit, was a few minutes' walk from the primary school. Pippa had hoped to put off formal childcare until Ruby could go to preschool, but there was simply too much work to do, and while Sheila was happy to take Ruby for an afternoon each week, Pippa didn't want to wear out her welcome. So two mornings at Little Puffins had become the norm.

Pippa delivered Ruby to Alicia, one of the assistants. 'Good morning, Ruby!' said Alicia, taking her hand. 'We're doing finger painting this morning. That'll be fun, won't it?'

Ruby stuck her fingers in her mouth in a passable imitation of a shy child.

'Bye bye Ruby, see you later,' said Pippa, bending to give her a kiss.

'Mummy!' cried Ruby, stretching out an imploring hand, her eyes wide and tragic. 'Don't go!'

Alicia raised a well-defined eyebrow.

'I'll see you after lunch, Ruby,' Pippa said quickly.

Ruby's eyes narrowed. 'What for lunch?' she asked Alicia.

'Why don't we go and look at the menu?' cooed Alicia. Ruby pulled her into the building without a backward glance.

'And now, school,' Pippa said to Freddie, marching him down the path at a brisk pace.

'Schooooool!' echoed Freddie, kicking up leaves on the pavement.

Pippa glanced at her watch. 'And we might even be on time.' She took Freddie's hand as the pavement ended. 'Stay close to the wall. That's right.'

Sure enough, the playground was full of parents talking in little groups and children weaving their way between them. The reception classrooms were at the back of the school, and as Pippa and Freddie navigated the islands of grown-ups and the streams of children, she saw her particular group; Lila, Caitlin, Imogen and Sam.

Caitlin waved. 'What time d'you call this?' she shouted.

'What do you mean?' said Pippa. 'I'm on time for once.'

'Exactly,' grinned Caitlin.

'Wait until yours can put up proper resistance,' said Pippa, looking at the stroller where Caitlin's younger one, Josh, was fast asleep. 'Ruby was working herself up this morning at the nursery door. If I hadn't distracted her with lunch I'd still be there.' She watched Freddie chasing Bella across the playground, shouting and puffing bubbles as he ran. 'Hang on a minute . . . why is Freddie the only child with a squeezy bottle?'

'Friday is rocket day,' said Lila. 'Bella actually remembered to tell me.'

'Gah!' Pippa ran her hands through her hair in despair, and immediately regretted it as Freddie's sticky hands had left their mark on hers. 'Freddie said it was today.'

'You're early,' said Lila. 'Brownie points from Miss Darcy.'

20

The bell rang and there was a general charge for the lining-up point, like iron filings to a magnet, until a long snake of children undulated before every classroom door. The children chatted, swapped cards and bounced balls, while all the parents' eyes were on the doors, waiting for the teachers to appear.

Year 2 began to file in, then year 1, as their doors opened. Then Miss Darcy's door creaked and the teaching assistant, Mrs Ridout, beckoned the reception class children in.

'They're always first,' grumbled a parent Pippa didn't know. 'Some of us have jobs to go to.' The other classroom door opened, and she closed her mouth and looked straight ahead.

Parents in suits took purposeful strides to the gate, while parents in jeans and gilets and jumpers drifted in the same direction. 'Coffee?' said Caitlin.

'I'd love to, but work,' said Pippa. 'Lady H calls.'

'Ooh yes,' said Lila. 'I was wondering about serving drinks in coconut shells. There are some very realistic ones online.'

'What does Jeff think?' asked Pippa, straight-faced.

Lila shrugged. 'Sometimes I don't think he's interested.'

'That's normal,' said Imogen. 'My other half said, "Just tell me where and when and I'll hire a morning suit."'

'S'pose,' said Lila. 'Doug was like that. But Jeff does shows all the time. I thought he'd be really into it and we'd plan it together, but every time I come up with something he goes "meh". Anyway, best get to work.'

'How's the experiment going?' Pippa asked.

'Great!' said Lila. 'He's getting lots done. New song arrangements, another residency, and all sorts.'

Lila had increased her working hours now that Bella was at school, and Jeff had cut his to four days a week, with the aim of devoting that day to increasing the bookings of his a capella group, Short Back and Sides.

'I'm glad it's working out,' said Pippa.

'He's getting a list of songs together for the wedding set,' said Lila. 'So far, that's his only contribution.' Her face clouded. 'I worry that we'll be there on the day in our ordinary clothes with a supermarket cake and a bunch of flowers from the petrol station.'

'I don't think it'll come to that,' said Pippa laughing. 'But I'd better dash to the Hall, or who knows where you'll get married.'

***

'There's an awful lot to think about,' said Lady Higginbotham, frowning. 'How many rooms do you think we should list on the form?'

'As many as we can,' said Pippa. 'Because if you add them later you have to pay again.'

Lady Higginbotham shuddered. 'I suppose. But how many of our rooms do you think people would actually want to get married in?'

'There's the morning room,' said Beryl. 'That's nice. And the dining room. You could fit heaps of people in there if you moved the table.'

'But where would the table go?' Lady Higginbotham looked utterly helpless, as if she would have to move it all

22

by herself.

'In a room we're not using that day,' said Beryl patiently. 'We can take the leaves out.' As Lady Higginbotham's housekeeper she would be in charge, and had already agreed to be the 'responsible person' for the venue, since her employer felt entirely inadequate.

'Oh well...' Lady Higginbotham sighed gently and waved a hand. 'Whatever you think is best, Pippa.'

'Morning room, dining room, drawing room?' Lady Higginbotham nodded. 'And the hallway? It's got a lovely floor and they could do photos on the grand staircase.'

'Ooh yes!' Beryl clasped her hands.

'How many chairs shall we need?' asked Lady Higginbotham, rather faintly. 'And what about staff?'

'We can hire all that,' said Pippa airily. 'Maybe we could get students from the local college to help out, for experience.'

'Mmm,' said Lady Higginbotham. 'I wonder how many weddings we could host in a year?' Was it the light, or was there a distinct gleam in her pale-blue eyes?

'Lots, I imagine,' said Pippa. 'Certainly once we're approved, and get on lists, and start advertising. And you know Lila wants to be your first victim, I mean wedding guest.'

'Yes!' Lady Higginbotham's eyes sparkled. 'We *must* get this form done.'

Pippa's phone buzzed, but she knew that Lady Higginbotham would look reproachful if she checked it. *It's probably only Lila wanting to change the theme to a 70s disco*, she consoled herself. 'Yes. We'll get the form

23

done today — I can do it online — and then we've really started.'

'Good.' Lady Higginbotham walked to her desk and switched on the computer, which looked as if it had time-travelled from an earlier decade. 'Let's go to work.'

An hour later, after various discussions which ended in Lady Higginbotham saying 'Whatever *you* think, dear,' and somehow always involved Pippa or Beryl doing the actual work, the form was on its way, with payment. 'There,' said Pippa, flexing her fingers. 'And now we wait.'

'They won't take long, will they?' asked Lady Higginbotham. 'I mean, we have a business to run here.'

'They'll have to send someone to inspect the Hall,' said Pippa. 'Once they're happy and we've provided the necessary certificates, we should be good to go.'

'Wonderful,' said Lady Higginbotham, happily. 'Do you think you could get some quotes together for a wedding brochure, Pippa? I mean, we do need to be prepared.' And the gleam in her eyes had returned.

Back in the Mini, Pippa checked her phone. The message was from Serendipity: *She's ringing every half-hour. Still haven't picked up. Can you tell her to GO AWAY? S*

Oh Suze, thought Pippa. *Do you have to do this?* She sighed and texted back. *Ignore her. If she can't talk to you, eventually she'll have to give up. P x*

She put the phone into the cupholder and started the engine, but as she did so, the phone rang.

It was a special ringtone which she had assigned to a particular person.

The theme to *Jaws*.

Pippa debated whether to answer it, but given that she would have to deal with this person sooner or later and there was no point in putting her off, she sighed and reached for the phone.

'Hello, Janey, what can I do for you?'

'I'm so glad I caught you,' purred Janey Dixon, as if Pippa were a particularly plump and juicy mouse. 'I have a little proposition for you.'

'Oh?' said Pippa, already thinking *no*.

'I happened to be speaking to Jim Horsley the other day and he mentioned that he was launching a neighbourhood lookout scheme, which sounds like *just* your sort of thing.'

'I'm not sure it does,' said Pippa. 'And besides, I've already said no.'

Jim Horsley had texted her, on his personal mobile, to ask her to pop into the police station and discuss it. *Would be fun to work together again*, he had written. It would be; but Pippa had no intention of getting tangled up with Jim Horsley. However blue his eyes were. Plus he had a girlfriend. So no. She had replied: *I don't think Much Gadding is a burglary hotspot, and people will stick their noses in anyway.*

I thought you'd be up for it, had flashed up moments later.

To which she had written: *I'm too busy to be up for anything.*

And if she could turn down Jim Horsley, she could certainly turn down Janey Dixon.

'Well if you won't be involved with that,' said Janey,

dismissively, 'how about your own weekly column in the *Chronicle*?'

Pippa nearly dropped the phone. 'My own column?'

'Yeeeees,' purred Janey. 'Like a sort of casebook of crimes you've investigated, and how you solved them. Insights into the criminal mind, that sort of thing. People love true crime, and the gorier the better.'

'You must be kidding, Janey,' said Pippa. 'OK, so I've had a part in clearing up some cases —'

'You're a local celebrity!' cried Janey.

'No I'm not. Four cases. Four events that I don't particularly want to relive, and the last one was over a year ago —'

'Not quite a year, I think you'll find,' said Janey, smoothly.

'Long enough. Anyway, I'm retired. I have literally no time for crime. So the answer's no.' Pippa paused. 'Now, if you wanted to ask me to do a column about life as an event organiser and PR person, with lots of lovely event photos —'

'You can buy advertising with the paper like the other businesses,' said Janey, and the phone went dead.

'*Ugh*,' said Pippa, to no-one, and switched on the radio. *Ooh good, Duran Duran.* She bawled along with 'Hungry Like The Wolf' as she trundled down the drive of Higginbotham Hall and onto the main road. If she was quick, she could get those brochure quotes before it was time to fetch her tragically abandoned child from the nursery and find out how much fun she'd had.

26

CHAPTER 4

'Ruby's been ever so good,' said Alicia, whose tabard now bore a bright green handprint. 'She ate everything, and painted a lovely picture. Didn't you, Ruby?'

Ruby nodded until her head looked ready to come off, and held up a picture of a forest. The leaves were thickly-applied green handprints, and the trunks wobbly streaks of brown with the occasional fingerprint splodged in.

'I like the bark effect,' said Pippa.

Alicia peered at the painting. 'Oh yes, I suppose it is.' She smiled. 'We meant to do that, of course.'

'I didn't doubt it for a second.' Pippa scrutinised her daughter. Her face was clean, but her T-shirt had suffered from both art and lunch. 'Fish pie?'

Alicia's eyes widened. 'It was!' She opened her mouth to speak, closed it, then opened it again. 'I hope you don't mind me asking, but . . . was it you who solved the —' She leaned in and mouthed '*murders*'.

'I helped out with a few, yes,' said Pippa, smiling. 'But

I'm retired now. All in the past.'

'That's good,' said Alicia, looking relieved. 'I mean, a quiet place like this, you don't expect it, do you?'

'No.' Pippa held out her hand and Ruby stumped over tetchily. 'See you on Monday, Alicia.'

As Pippa suspected, Ruby was rubbing her eyes by the time they got home. She administered a sippy cup of milk and put Ruby down for a nap, and for a wonder, Ruby didn't argue.

And lunch for me, thought Pippa, making herself a ham sandwich. At least she wouldn't have to eat it at a rate of one bite every few minutes, so that the last half of the sandwich was stale by the time she reached it. She switched the kettle on and as she did so, her phone pinged.

Serendipity: *Please help, Pippa, they're here and I'm trapped in the bedroom*

What?!? Pippa texted back. *What do you mean? Who's there? Are they in your house? Should I phone 999?* She imagined Serendipity hiding under the bed, shielding the light from her phone, while burglars shone torches into every corner and unhooked her paintings from the walls to look for a safe.

My family are outside and they aren't going away.

'Aarrgh!' cried Pippa.

'Mummy!' wailed Ruby. 'Stop shouting!'

'Right.' Pippa ran upstairs and picked Ruby up. 'I'll drive you to sleep, Ruby. Come on, we'll go for a spin. I'll tuck you up in a blanket.'

28

Ruby stared at her. 'Like a 'venture?'

'That's right, Ruby, an adventure.'

Pippa settled her in the car and drove the few minutes to River Lane and her former home, Rosebud Cottage. The cottage was almost hidden by an enormous black Range Rover. Pippa parked the Mini outside the next house, checked Ruby was asleep, and got out.

A woman in a silky moss-green top and white jeans, with blonde hair which didn't move at all, was peering through the letterbox. 'Dippy, come out! I know you're in there!' By her side was a tall, slim young woman in a Barbour jacket and Hunter wellies, and at the wheel of the Range Rover was a man with thinning dark hair, wearing a blazer and what appeared to be a regimental tie.

'*Dippy!*' The woman huffed and let the flap of the letterbox bang shut, then thumped on the door. Finally she turned, muttering, and caught sight of Pippa. 'Are you the neighbour?' she asked, smiling sweetly.

'You could say that,' said Pippa. 'She isn't in, you're wasting your time.'

'Her car's here,' said the young woman, pointing at Serendipity's battered Citroen 2CV.

'Exactly, Minty,' said the first woman. 'Her rustbucket is here so she must be too. The silly girl,' she added, raising her voice.

'Are you Serendipity's mother?' asked Pippa.

'That's right.' She held out a tanned hand with peach nails and several dangerous-looking rings. 'Julia Skeffington-Jones. *Not* plain Jones, as Dippy calls herself.'

Pippa stifled the thought that burglars in Serendipity's

house might have been easier to deal with. At least you could set the police on them.

'I'm Araminta,' said the younger woman, 'Minty for short.'

'Hello, Minty,' said Pippa, shaking the proffered hand, which wasn't nearly as well-cared for as her mother's. 'Is Serendipity expecting you?'

'She ought to be,' said Julia Skeffington-Jones darkly. 'She knows we want to talk to her, and she won't answer the phone to our PR lady. *She*, by the way, told us that Dippy had got some *assistant* to do her dirty work.'

'Did she now,' said Pippa, grimly.

'Can you believe it? So Suzanne suggested a direct approach might be better. She's ever so good. Very experienced. Very professional.'

'So she suggested that doorstepping your daughter and shouting through her letterbox would work,' said Pippa, deadpan.

'Well, if she would *open the door and listen to me*, we'd get somewhere.'

'She can't,' said Pippa. 'She's out, I tell you.'

'When will she be back?' asked the man in the car, presumably Serendipity's father. 'It's Rotary night, we can't stay here for ever.'

'I couldn't say,' said Pippa. 'I'm not her assistant.'

'Is she usually out at this time? Do *you* know where she is?' Serendipity's mother, scenting blood, gave Pippa a gimletty look.

'Nope,' said Pippa. 'I can pass a message on if I see her, but that's all I can do.' She opened the door of the

Mini to make her exit, then realised that she was stuck. If she drove off now, they'd know that she'd come to talk to them, and presumably that Serendipity had called her, and therefore knew they were there. *Oh heck*. Then a thought popped into her head. She closed the car door, walked the few yards to Wisteria Cottage, and knocked.

Marge emerged, bearing a large frying-pan. 'What *now* oh hello Pippa.'

'Can I come in and bring Ruby?' Pippa muttered. 'Serendipity's under house arrest and I can't leave the scene.'

'Yes, I've got the stock pot you wanted,' said Marge, loudly. 'Why don't you come in and have a cuppa?'

'I'd love to,' Pippa shouted. 'I'll just get Ruby.' She ran to the Mini and wrestled a sleepy and protesting Ruby out of her car seat. 'You can't stay there, honey, we're going to visit Auntie Marge.'

Ruby screwed her fists into her eyes as Pippa bore her away, not daring to look at the trio outside Serendipity's house. She was only conscious of breathing again once Marge's front door was shut and locked behind her.

'House arrest, eh?' asked Marge, walking into her narrow kitchen and switching the kettle on. 'That definitely calls for tea.'

'I know.' Pippa cuddled Ruby into her shoulder. 'That bunch are Serendipity's family, and they're trying to winkle her out and make her do a reality show.'

'Ahhh.' Marge went to root in her hall cupboard and returned with a small box of picture books. 'Now, would these be of interest to Miss Ruby?'

Ruby stretched out her hands to the box. Pippa popped her, still wrapped in her blanket, into the corner of the sofa and put the box of board books beside her. Marge's cat Beyoncé jumped onto the sofa, sniffed the box, then walked to the opposite end and began to wash herself thoroughly.

Pippa pulled out her phone. 'I'll text Serendipity and let her know I'm here.' *On the scene and have seen your parents. Decamped to Marge. Your father wants to go to Rotary.*

A reply came quickly. *Ooh good. Are they moving?*

Pippa crept to the window and peeped through the net curtains. Minty was leaning on the car, picking her nails, while her mother was hugging her elbows, shifting from foot to foot. *They look bored*, she replied.

Suddenly Julia Skeffington-Jones's head shot up. 'That's it, I've had enough.' She stalked to the door of Rosebud Cottage and raised the flap of the letterbox. 'We're going, Dippy. I can't stand here all day waiting for you to finish sulking.'

'Way to go,' muttered Pippa.

'Please think it over.' She let the flap fall and walked away. Then she turned back and opened the letterbox again. 'We still love you, Dippy,' she said, and her voice trembled. She walked down the path, taking her mobile phone from her bag, and got into the car without a backward glance.

'About flaming time,' said Marge, making Pippa jump. 'They've been hanging around for the best part of an hour, shouting. I thought they might be some sort of cult. Or stalkers, maybe.'

Pippa gawped at Marge. 'Craft stalkers? Seriously?'

Marge shrugged. 'Could happen.'

The car engine started and the Range Rover moved off, negotiating the sharp bend into the main road with difficulty.

Pippa's thumbs flew over her keyboard. *They've gone.*

Oh thank heavens. Can I come in?

Pippa showed the message to Marge. 'Course she can,' said Marge.

Marge says yes.

Pippa pressed *Send,* then looked up from her phone.

Hide!

Minty's tall, slender figure was just visible at the top of River Lane. The Range Rover was nowhere to be seen, but Pippa suspected it was lurking, ready to reverse and possibly ram-raid Rosebud Cottage once Serendipity's presence was verified.

Back in the bedroom, Serendipity texted. *I don't believe this.*

'How sneaky was that?' said Pippa.

'Very sneaky,' said Marge. 'I'm impressed.'

'Hmmm.' Pippa thought over Julia Skeffington-Jones's actions — the final appeal to her daughter, walking away, pulling out her phone — 'Suze told them to do that. I'd put money on it.' Her fingers tightened on her phone.

'What you doing, Mummy?' asked Ruby, looking up from her book.

'Observing, Ruby.'

'Why you ozzerving?'

Minty's head was down. Probably texting her mother.

Stay put, Pippa told Serendipity. *I think Minty's communicating with the mothership. May be seeking instruction from General Suze.*

They waited. Minty's gaze remained on her hands. Then she shrugged, waved at the cottage, and left.

She's going, said Pippa, *but leave it 2 mins.*

'I'll go out and make sure they've hooked it,' said Marge, grimly. Picking up her frying pan, she bustled out, leaving the front door open. A minute later, a gong-like sound echoed round River Lane as Marge whacked the cast-iron pan on a metal lamp-post.

All clear I think, texted Pippa.

In an instant the door of Rosebud Cottage banged and Serendipity sprinted towards Marge's house. 'Oh my gosh,' she panted, leaning on the sitting-room door frame.

Ruby surveyed her, wide-eyed. 'Why you running?' she asked.

Serendipity got most of her breath back before answering. 'My parents came round and I was hiding. I don't want them to see me.'

Ruby frowned. 'Naughty,' she said, and returned to her book.

'No it isn't,' said Serendipity, indignantly. 'They want me to do something and I *won't.*'

Ruby considered, head on one side. 'Naughty,' she concluded, running her finger along a line of text.

Marge came in and closed the door behind her. 'Now then, what's going on, Serendipity? What's all this about a TV show?'

'It's to pay for a new roof,' said Serendipity. 'And once Mummy has a bee in her bonnet, she won't let go.'

'Maybe she'll get stung then,' said Marge.

'Oh no, she fancies a career as a media celebrity,' said Serendipity, flumping down beside Ruby. 'Apparently if I can do it, anyone can.'

'Did she actually say that?' cried Pippa.

'More or less. I mean, it was couched in Mummy-speak and "dear" and "darling", but that was the gist of it.'

'Oof. No wonder you're digging your heels in.'

'Does that mean I'm being unreasonable?' Serendipity's voice had risen, and there was a spark of fire in her usually serene gaze.

'No, no,' Pippa soothed.

'Maybe,' said Marge, and grinned as her guests goggled at her. 'Your mother's acting like a spoilt child because she can't have what she wants. And as our wise Ruby said, you're acting like a naughty one because you don't want to face up to her. You can carry on doing that, or you can find a way to be the grown-up.'

'Oh, Marge,' said Serendipity, and put her face in her hands. 'Why can't she just behave?' she wailed, somewhat muffled.

'I'll make tea,' said Marge, and bustled out.

Serendipity stared at Pippa, looking almost as tragic as Ruby had that morning. 'What am I going to do?'

'Sleep on it,' said Pippa. 'Don't take any calls, not from your mother and definitely not from Suze.' She scowled. 'I'll deal with her myself.'

35

CHAPTER 5

'Could I have a word, Mrs Parker?'

Oh no, thought Pippa. At least it couldn't be lateness, as she had managed to be on time not once, but *twice* that school day. Her brain flipped through the possibilities. Freddie had definitely taken his PE kit in after the weekend, and she had put his homework book in his bag herself, as well as filling out his reading diary the requisite three times. And now here was Miss Darcy, looking slightly nervous, whose eyes had been fixed on her as she approached the reception classroom door.

'Of course,' she said, and braced herself.

'I wanted to let you know how pleased I am with Freddie's progress. He's a very imaginative boy.'

'I suppose he is,' said Pippa, thoughtfully.

'Oh, he is. I asked the children to draw a superhero today, and do you know what he came up with?'

'I have no idea,' said Pippa.

'A moose!' Miss Darcy smiled broadly. 'And it had all

sorts of useful things in its antlers. I thought that was so clever. Is he fond of nature?'

Pippa thought of Freddie shrimping with Marge in the River Gad. 'Oh yes,' she said.

'Wonderful,' said Miss Darcy. 'Freddie will be my Star of the Week for imagination and effort.' She beamed, then turned to call Freddie.

'Sipadipity was naughty,' said Ruby, apropos of nothing. 'She ran away.'

'Oh dear,' said Miss Darcy to her. 'Imagination must run in the family,' she observed.

'It's quite possible. Come along, Freddie.' And Pippa departed with a child in either hand.

***

'You look as if you want to beat someone up,' said Simon, when he arrived home. 'I hope it isn't me.'

'Not this time,' said Pippa, kissing him. 'Although you're late, and you didn't let me know.'

'I'm sorry.' Simon took off his tie and hung it on the stair-post, then tightened it into a noose. 'Impromptu brainstorming session at the Coach and Horses. And yes, I stuck to Diet Coke.'

'The Coach and Horses? But that's nowhere near your work.'

'That's why we went there.'

'Why so cloak and dagger?'

'Tell you later.' Simon went into the lounge to say hello to the children, who were in their pyjamas and watching some creative inspiration, as Pippa had decided to rename the TV.

Once Ruby and Freddie were settled, Pippa came downstairs to pursue the matter. 'So, the Coach and Horses. Isn't that the other side of Gadcester?'

'It is. By an amazing coincidence, it's almost exactly the same distance from our HQ and the HQ of the firm we want to take over. Oh, and equally difficult to get to.'

'And?'

Simon stared at the weather forecast for a few moments. 'And so that's where Declan and I met.'

'*Declan*?'

'Mm-hm,' said Simon, watching a cold front spread over the north of England.

'Declan who used to be your boss? Declan I'll-get-you-to-do-all-the-stuff-I-can't-be-bothered-with Declan? Declan who jumped ship at exactly the wrong time Declan?'

'That's him.' Simon muted the television. 'He works for the other firm. He moved there once the competition clause in his contract ended.'

'Just you and Declan? No-one else?'

'I went for a quiet drink with an old colleague and friend. And this reaction is exactly why we went off the beaten track.'

Pippa exhaled. 'I worry that he'll stitch you up.'

'He won't. He just wanted to get the lie of the land. There have been rumours floating around, and he figured I'd tell him the truth.'

'Did you?'

The local weather was on now, and from the silent gestures of the presenter, there might be a hurricane brewing. 'I told him as much as I thought he should know.'

Pippa raised an eyebrow. 'Ever thought of going into politics?'

'Ha!' Simon put the sound back on. 'I'd get eaten alive.' They endured an advert for drain cleaner in silence. 'Anyway, what about you? How was your day?'

'Odd,' said Pippa. 'Dragooned by Lady H, propositioned by Janey Dixon, thwarted a house arrest, and discovered our son is a creative genius.'

'I wish my life was that exciting,' said Simon. 'Is Freddie a creative genius?'

'His teacher doesn't watch *MegaMoose*, so yes he is.'

'All right. Who was under house arrest?'

'Serendipity. And I'm still fuming. Her family is *awful*.'

'Aren't most families?'

Pippa considered. 'When you have to live with them, maybe. But they're not usually awful in front of other people. Poor Serendipity was trapped in her own home.' She paused. 'Her mother calls her Dippy.'

Simon grimaced. 'OK, you've convinced me.'

'And Suze is behind it. I swear she was directing operations. They doubled back to try and catch us out, but luckily I was watching.'

'I'm imagining you in the bushes with a walkie talkie.'

'In Marge's front room with a mobile phone, actually.' Pippa snorted. 'Marge thinks Serendipity should stand up to her mother, but the way she's behaving... Suze isn't helping. I could *kill* her. All this to land a deal for her client. There are boundaries, you know.'

39

Simon put his arm round Pippa in the soothing way which particularly irritated her. 'Of course. Have you spoken to Suze? Or emailed her?'

'No, I haven't. I don't trust myself not to shout at her, and if she sees that she's getting to me it'll make her worse. She's like a dog with a bone. Or a shark when it scents blood. Speaking of which, steak for dinner?'

'Yes please.' Simon frowned. 'I haven't forgotten our anniversary, have I?'

'You'd know by now if you had. I just have the urge to sink my teeth into something bloody.'

Simon winced. 'Medium rare for me, please.'

'Potato wedges all right?'

'Oh yes.'

Pippa mutilated potatoes and put them in the oven to cook, then came back through. Someone she vaguely recognised as a D-list celebrity was being interviewed on a sofa. Maybe that would be Serendipity's mother in a few months. If she could get her show without Serendipity on board. *Over my dead body is she signing up to that thing.*

Her phone sang out. *Suze.*

Pippa stared at it, then stabbed at the *Answer* button.

'Round one to you,' said Suze, sounding amused. Unfortunately my client wasn't disposed to hang around, or I'm sure we could have got a result.'

'Smoked my friend out, you mean.'

Simon raised his eyebrows. 'Guess who,' said Pippa, and he made a face. 'I'll take it in the kitchen. There's no sense in ruining your night too.'

'It isn't personal, Pip,' said Suze.

'So why are you ringing me in the evening?'

'I thought you would be busy with child stuff earlier.' Suze paused. 'And maybe even work.'

'Just because I don't work fourteen hours a day that doesn't mean I don't take my job seriously,' snapped Pippa. 'And at least I have a sense of professional ethics.'

'Jolly good,' said Suze. 'Well done you.'

'Stop being so bloody patronising!' cried Pippa. 'And if you think this approach will work, you're wrong.'

Her phone beeped.

'We'll see,' said Suze. 'I usually get what I want in the end. And besides, you do owe me a favour. More than one, in fact.'

Pippa almost laughed. 'Do I? I don't think so.'

'Oh, you do. Remember Dev Hardman? I gave you a plum celebrity for your little fete, and you've never repaid me.'

'He ruined the whole fete! And he only came because it fitted in with his own plans. So if that's your idea of a favour, you'll be better off if I don't repay it.'

Beep beep.

Pippa removed the phone from her ear and stared at it. 'Call waiting,' she said, and pressed the button to take the call, relieved to have a break from Suze.

'Pippa,' said a hoarse voice.

'Who is this?'

There was no response but ragged breathing. 'Look, if you're some kind of pervert I'm really not in the mood. Tell me who this is, or I'll hang up.'

'*Ahhh!*' Pippa screwed her mouth up. *Honestly.* Did

people have nothing better to do? She was about to switch back to Suze and shout at her for light relief when she realised that *Ahhh* sounded as if the person was in pain.

'Are you all right? Do you need help?'

The breathing on the other end of the line seemed to be working up to something. Pippa longed to fire off questions, but she sensed the person was in no fit state to answer them. Where were they calling from? And why her? She waited, questions buzzing round her head.

'Iss J—' A cough broke off the sentence.

'J? J who?' *Julia? Julia Skeffington-Jones?* Was she looking for sympathy? Had Suze put her up to this? *If you have, Suze, I'll report you to your professional body —*

'Janey.'

'Janey Dixon?' Incredulity hit Pippa like a bucket of cold water. This croaking, coughing voice was nothing like the annoying reporter Pippa knew. 'Where are you?'

More breathing, becoming more ragged.

'Please tell me where you are so I can help you!'

'Pass help,' Janey said thickly.

'I can send an ambulance if you'll only tell me where you are!' Pippa felt a tear drop off her chin. She hadn't even known she was crying.

Simon came in. 'What on earth is wrong?' he said, staring at Pippa. 'Do you need me to speak to Suze?'

Pippa shook her head. 'Not that,' she choked out.

'Ven muh.'

Simon folded her in his arms. 'Please tell me what's wrong, Pip.'

'Venge muh.'

42

'*Avenge me?*' said Pippa.

'Yeh,' said Janey Dixon.

'Please tell me where you're calling from!'

Beep beep. Suze was waiting. Pippa pushed the button to end Suze's call. 'Please, Janey, speak to me!'

'Can you see what number she's calling from?' asked Simon. 'Shall I call an ambulance? Or the police?'

Pippa tried to focus on the screen through her tears. 'It's a mobile. She could be anywhere.'

'Maybe the police can trace it. I'll ring them.' Simon gave her a final squeeze and hurried to the phone in the hall.

'Hang on Janey, we're tracing your call and then we can get an ambulance to you.'

No response. Not even breathing.

'Janey? Janey!'

But Janey Dixon spoke no more.

CHAPTER 6

'Don't end the call!' Simon shouted. 'They're tracing it.'

Pippa listened for a few seconds longer. 'I — I think she's gone.' Slowly, she put the phone on the table.

'They've got the approximate area.' Simon came into the room and looked at Pippa, and his face was serious. 'It's the centre of Gadcester. A block on Station Street.'

'That's where the newspaper office is. Tell them she's probably there.'

Simon relayed the information, then listened. 'An ambulance is on the way.' He paused. 'They're asking if you'll go.'

Pippa could feel the blood drain from her face. 'Me?'

'She rang you. And —' He screwed his face up in an effort to get the words out. 'They may need someone to identify her…'

The roads were quiet at this time, and Pippa felt very alone as she drove down the dark country lane to Gadcester. She had switched the radio off as the noise was too jarring, and the car was silent. Her hands trembled on the steering wheel, and she had to blink hard every so often to clear the film of water which cloaked her eyes.

But at last there were outlying cottages, and streetlights, and soon she was driving past satellite estates and business parks and into Gadcester. Station Street was right in the centre, and as she turned into the street the first thing she saw was flashing blue lights. An ambulance was outside the square red-brick newspaper offices, and a police car, and a security van on the other side of the road.

PC Gannet was standing at the door to the building. 'Mrs Parker,' he said, with no expression at all.

'Do I go in?' Pippa asked.

'They're on the first floor,' said PC Gannet, which she took to be a yes. 'Don't touch *anything*.'

'I won't,' said Pippa, and he held the door open for her.

Pippa walked through the deserted reception area and up a steel-and-glass staircase. It clanged, and the sound echoed around her. Above she could hear voices, and when she reached the landing, she followed them to a closed door. She swallowed, and knocked.

Inspector Fanshawe's face appeared in the glass panel and he opened the door. 'Mrs Parker, thanks for coming. Stay back, if you would. The paramedics are doing their best.'

Pippa took in a knot of green uniforms crouching, hiding something. 'Is she…?'

'They're doing their best,' the inspector repeated.

One of the paramedics turned. 'We'll take her to the hospital. CPR's doing nothing, and the blood loss —'

'We found a handbag near where the — she was lying,' said Inspector Fanshawe. 'It has a purse with bank cards for Ms J Dixon.'

Two paramedics unfolded a stretcher and Pippa looked away. 'One, two, three.'

'Do you know if she was married? If she had any family?'

Pippa shook her head. 'I have no idea. I literally met her once.'

The inspector frowned. 'Then why did she phone you?'

'Can you get the door?' one of the paramedics called.

Pippa and the inspector held open a door each, and the paramedics hurried over with the stretcher. Even in the half-second it took them to get past, Pippa had seen curly blonde hair matted with blood, smudged red lipstick, and the sharp, and now very very pale features of Janey Dixon.

'That's her,' she said softly. 'What happened? How did she —'

'It's pretty gruesome,' said Inspector Fanshawe. 'Are you sure you want me to tell you?'

'I don't,' said Pippa. 'But of all the people she could have phoned, she phoned me. She asked me to avenge her.'

Inspector Fanshawe stared. 'She said what?'

'*Avenge me*. That was all she managed to say.'

Inspector Fanshawe continued to stare. 'So you feel it's your mission?'

Pippa met his gaze until he broke it. 'Not exactly, but — she wanted me to be involved. And she knew she was dying. She said *past help*.'

The inspector sighed. 'She was probably right, too. Are

you sure —'

'*Yes.*'

'Very well. When we got in here Janey Dixon was lying face-down, next to her handbag, with her mobile phone beside her.'

'It must have fallen from her hand —'

'And there was a trail of blood which started at one of the filing cabinets, opposite the door. A few feet in length.'

'But what —'

'Do you see that glass case?' Inspector Fanshawe pointed to a wood-framed case mounted on the wall, under the clock.

'Yes, but . . . it's empty.'

'It is. There's a brass plate on that case which tells me what's usually in there. It says "The original editorial spike of the *Gadcester Chronicle*. In use until 1987."' He swallowed. 'I imagine you can guess where it ended up. In Janey Dixon's back.'

Pippa shuddered.

'I'm sorry, but you did ask —'

'No, no. Thank you for telling me.'

'I'm sure I don't need to tell you that this is a crime scene. Forensics will arrive any minute to do their job, dust for fingerprints, all that...' He glanced at Pippa. 'But there is something I want to share with you. Something odd.' He pointed to the carpet by the filing cabinet, where the trail of blood began. 'Do you see that square grey thing?'

Pippa took a careful step. 'Yes. What is it? It looks like...'

'A letter from a computer keyboard,' said Inspector

Fanshawe. 'I've checked her keyboard, and the ones nearby, and I can't see any missing letters. That suggests this has been brought in specially. We'll check for prints, obviously, but I don't expect to find any.'

Pippa's head was spinning. 'But why would anyone… What letter is it?'

'*A*,' said Inspector Fanshawe, grimly. 'Like Exhibit A.'

***

Pippa sipped from a plastic cup of scalding, gritty coffee, and shifted on the hard plastic chair. Her phone said *9.43*.

'Go home,' Inspector Fanshawe had said. 'There's nothing you can do till the morning.'

'There is,' said Pippa. 'I can go to the hospital.'

'Yes.' The inspector's gaze was steady. 'But I don't think it'll be good news.'

'Me neither.' Pippa took her car keys from her bag. 'There doesn't seem to be anyone else, though. And it's wrong for her to be on her own.'

'It's a good thought.' The inspector patted her shoulder. 'Mind how you go, and watch out for the drunks in A&E.' He coughed. 'I'll try and get in touch with the editor of the *Chronicle*, see if he can come up with a friend or relative. Not that you're not —'

'I'm not,' said Pippa, 'but I'll have to do.'

The Accident and Emergency department at Gadcester General Hospital was quiet, possibly because it was a weeknight. Two young women were waiting, one with a swollen ankle, and an old man in a cap sat opposite Pippa, coughing violently every thirty seconds or so. Pippa

48

wondered if he was there for the cough, or something else.

A nurse with a clipboard came into the waiting room and everyone looked up. 'Mrs Parker?' she asked.

'Yes?' said Pippa. The old man tutted, which set him off coughing again.

'If you'd like to come through.'

'How is she?' asked Pippa.

'The doctor will be here in a moment,' said the nurse, leading her down the corridor to another waiting area.

The moment lasted a very long time. Pippa gazed at the abstract art on the walls, the red second hand of the clock sweeping round and round, the signs on the doors —

The door on the right opened and a man in scrubs came out. Pippa stood up. 'Mrs Parker? I'm Dr Simpkins.' He was tall, broad, in his thirties. He looked like a rugby player in a doctor's outfit. 'I'm afraid it isn't good news.'

Fast, loud footsteps were approaching. A lean man in a jumper and corduroy trousers was striding towards them. 'I'm Gerald Tamblyn, editor of the *Gadcester Chronicle*. I understand that one of my employees is here. Can I see her?'

Dr Simpkins didn't appear impressed. 'Mr Tamblyn, how did you get in?'

'Followed my nose,' said Gerald Tamblyn, tapping it.

'Would you happen to have contact details for Ms Dixon's family?' asked the doctor.

'Don't think there are any. Not married, no kids, never talked about family. Wasn't from round here originally, you see. You could say the newspaper was her family.' Gerald Tamblyn smiled a chummy smile. 'There was an ex-

49

partner, but that was a few years back.'

'I see,' said the doctor.

'So how is she?' asked the journalist. 'I only picked up the message half an hour ago, I was out at a friend's.' He looked keenly at the doctor, and his smile faded. 'She's dead, isn't she?' He paced up and down, running his hands through his sandy hair. 'Oh my. *Oh* my.'

'Is she?' Pippa asked quietly.

'Are you a friend of hers?' asked the doctor, under his breath.

Pippa paused. 'Yes. She phoned me when she was… I identified her.'

'I see.' Gerald Tamblyn pulled out a mobile phone. 'You can't use that here,' said the doctor. 'If you must, please return to reception.' The journalist strode off, muttering something about the front page.

The doctor turned back to Pippa. 'I'm afraid your friend's injury was very deep. The — weapon pierced a lung, causing tension pneumothorax. With the blood loss, and the time that must have elapsed before she was found, there was nothing anyone could have done. We couldn't revive her.'

'I see,' said Pippa. 'Thank you.'

'Would you like to see her?' The doctor indicated the door.

Pippa shook her head. 'I'd rather remember her as she was.' She sat down and ran her hands over her face.

Poor Janey. What a way to die.

'I'll, um, let you have a few minutes alone,' said the doctor, and went quietly through the door.

They'll be busy at the newspaper offices, thought Pippa. She imagined police officers in overalls putting clues into bags with tweezers, on their hands and knees examining strands of hair and bits of dust on the carpet, dusting drawer handles for prints. Speaking of the police... She dug her phone and the scrap of paper the Inspector had given her out of her bag, and walked back to the reception.

They couldn't save her, she texted. *The editor's here.*

And he was, talking into his phone. 'They already told me they've sealed it off. So we'll be on laptops. I just hope it isn't the whole building. If not, we could all go in the boardroom on the top floor. No, I don't know how long it'll take them to finish...'

Life goes on, thought Pippa. *More so for some people.* She headed for the glass doors.

'Wait!' Gerald Tamblyn cried. 'I didn't get your name! Can you give me a quote?'

'No,' said Pippa, and walked out.

CHAPTER 7

The room was light by the time Pippa woke. She felt cold air at her back and groped behind her in panic, then heard the sound of the kettle downstairs, and relaxed.

She had driven home quickly the night before, worried that lingering in the car park would give Gerald Tamblyn a chance to find her car, take the registration and somehow track her down. All the way home she checked her rear-view mirror for a car following her; but none did. The road was quiet.

There'll be a post-mortem, she thought, and wished she didn't have quite such a good working knowledge of criminal matters.

Simon had waited up for her, made cocoa with plenty of sugar in it, and held her while she choked out what she knew. 'I'm so sorry, Pip,' he said, 'I don't know what else to say.'

'She didn't have anyone,' said Pippa, sniffing.

'You did say she wasn't very nice,' Simon said, softly.

Pippa gave him a shocked glance. 'Lots of people aren't, but they still have family.'

'I know.' He stroked her back. 'Try not to think about it. There's nothing you can do until tomorrow.'

'Tomorrow...' Pippa let him lead her upstairs. 'I don't even want to think about what I might find out tomorrow.'

And now it was tomorrow. Pippa reached for her phone and stared at the black screen. Then she remembered she'd switched it off, and put it down. Whatever was lurking in there could wait until she'd had a cup of tea.

Simon arrived with mugs. 'What will you do today?' he asked, in a casual-seeming way.

Pippa accepted her mug and took a long slurp. 'Freddie to school. Ruby to playgroup.'

'And...?' Simon got into bed beside her.

'I'm not sure what else. I suppose it depends.'

'On what?'

Pippa shrugged. 'On whether I'm needed. I hope I'm not. I hope the forensics people find prints or DNA and match them.'

Simon looked at her and put his mug down. 'But you don't think they will, do you?'

Pippa shook her head. 'This wasn't a spur-of-the-moment thing. It was planned. The letter *A* the inspector found tells me that... It reminds me of something, but I can't think what.'

'It could just have been a sick joke,' said Simon. 'By someone too clever for their own good. And they're the sort of people who get caught out.'

The phone pealed downstairs. 'I'll get it,' said Simon,

tying his dressing gown more tightly round him.

He returned a couple of minutes later holding the receiver, with his hand over the speaker. 'It's PC Horsley.'

Pippa blinked. 'What the —?'

'He wants to know if you're all right,' said Simon, drily.

'Oh,' said Pippa, looking at the phone as if it might jump at her. 'Can you tell him I'm fine?'

'Sure,' said Simon. 'She says she's fine,' he said into the phone. 'It's early, so — Yes, I'll pass that on. Bye.' He pressed the button and tossed the phone onto the bed. 'Apparently he tried your mobile but that was off.'

'How did he know?' murmured Pippa. 'Unless the inspector told him. But why would he? It happened in Gadcester.'

Simon picked up his mobile and typed. 'Ah,' he said, and held the phone out to Pippa.

It was the *Gadcester Chronicle*'s Facebook stream. *BIZARRE MURDER OF TOP COLUMNIST*, it said, above a picture of Janey Dixon which was, Pippa judged, about ten years old. *Mystery woman helping police with their enquiries.*

Pippa made a noise and gave the phone back to Simon. 'That makes me sound like a suspect. And I'm not a mystery woman.'

'You are to the editor,' said Simon.

'I'm going to text the inspector,' said Pippa, picking up her own phone and switching it on. 'He needs to know what's on social media. At this rate, Gerald Whatsits will find himself in trouble.'

'Mmm,' said Simon. 'I'd guess he has a good idea

where the line is.'

'In my opinion,' said Pippa, thumbs flying. 'he's crossed it.' She pressed *Send* and gave a little *humph* of satisfaction. That was followed by a groan, as she read her messages.

Piglet: *Pippa, are you involved with this Janey Dixon thing? I have a feeling you are. Please reply. Jim.*

I must remember to change his contact name, thought Pippa, scrolling.

Suze: *Most people finish their calls. It was very rude of you to keep me on the line and then end the call like that. Not impressed.*

Tough. Pippa scrolled again.

A number without a name attached. *Just a heads-up. We checked the door-pass mechanism. Whoever did it left at 7.02pm using Janey Dixon's own pass. Inspector F.*

Pippa stared into space.

'What is it?' asked Simon.

'The killer's smart,' said Pippa. 'They think things through. And whether I want to be or not, I think I'm involved.'

***

Pippa's phone rang on the way to school, *Gadcester Police,* said the display. She pressed *Accept.* 'Hello, Pippa Parker.'

'Ahem, Mrs Parker,' corrected PC Gannet, clearing his throat. 'Would you be able to give a statement at Gadcester station today? I don't think I need to explain why.'

'You don't,' said Pippa. 'And it depends on whether I can find someone to mind my daughter.'

'This is important —'

'I know it is. I'll phone back.' And Pippa ended the call.

'No playgroup?' moaned Ruby, mouth turned down.

'Of course playgroup,' said Pippa, squeezing her hand. 'Mummy might have to go and do something for a little while.'

'You did something in the night,' said Ruby. 'I woke up, and Daddy came. He said you doing something.'

Pippa wondered whether she should recruit her daughter to help the police. 'I was. But you come first.'

At school she buttonholed Caitlin. 'Would you be able to watch Ruby at playgroup? I have — something urgent to do.'

Caitlin's eyes narrowed. 'Is this about…' She leaned in. '*Janey Dixon?*' she mouthed.

'Maybe,' said Pippa. 'Can't say.'

'Course I will,' said Caitlin. 'If you like I'll take her now, and she can have lunch at ours.'

'Thanks, you're a star.'

'I know,' said Caitlin. 'You owe me a playdate and cake.'

'Fair enough.'

Pippa bought a copy of the *Gadcester Chronicle* after she had dropped Freddie off, but there was nothing about the events of yesterday. *Of course there won't be, you fool,* she reproached herself. *There won't have been time.*

And if the office was cordoned off, would there even be an edition tomorrow?

Pippa phoned the police station to confirm her

availability, and set off for Gadcester. The roads out of Much Gadding were busy, full of harried parents rushing to get to work, and the traffic was on the slow side all the way to Gadcester. Pippa parked at the station, turned her phone to silent, and walked in.

She didn't have to wait long. Within two minutes of her arrival PC Horsley had appeared. 'P — Mrs Parker, if you'd like to come this way.'

'How come you're here?' Pippa asked, as they walked down the corridor. Not that she was sorry to see him. Far better to give a statement to Jim Horsley than nervy young PC Gannet.

Jim Horsley looked straight ahead while formulating his answer. 'The inspector thinks this'll be a big case. Obviously, the papers are already on to it. So he's calling in extras to Gadcester, and I'm one of them.' He opened the door to an interview room and waved Pippa in. 'Plus we've worked together before.'

'What, you and the inspector?' Pippa took a seat and reached for the jug of water and a glass.

'No, you and me.'

Water slopped over the rim of the glass. 'I beg your pardon?' asked Pippa, staring.

'Let's face it,' said Jim Horsley, handing her a paper towel to mop up the spill, 'you're already involved. Janey Dixon rang you. She could have rung anyone, including the police or an ambulance, but she chose you.'

'Anything the inspector didn't tell you?' asked Pippa.

Jim Horsley shrugged. 'He's given me the bare facts. The rest I can work out for myself. And you'll want to be part of the case.'

'You both seem very sure of that,' said Pippa, settling in her chair. 'All right, let's get on with this.'

Jim Horsley raised his eyebrows, opened his notebook, and switched on the recorder.

'This is the recording of an interview with Mrs Pippa Parker concerning the murder of Ms Janey Dixon, conducted on Thursday the fourth of October 2018, beginning nine-forty. Mrs Parker, please can you confirm your name, date of birth and address, and then I would like you to tell me, in your own words, what happened on the evening of Wednesday the third of October.'

Pippa described the bizarre phone call she had had from Janey Dixon.

'Are you fairly sure that what you've said were her exact words?' asked the policeman.

Pippa hesitated. 'Well, I was upset — it's not a normal situation to find yourself in. I was trying so hard to get Janey to tell me where she was that I possibly didn't concentrate on what she was saying, just whether or not it would help me find her.'

'But you're sure she never mentioned a name?'

'No. She never mentioned a person.'

'Mm.' PC Horsley scribbled a note. 'Had you spoken to Ms Dixon recently?'

'Yes.' Pippa frowned as she tried to remember when that had happened. 'In fact, I think it was yesterday morning. Can I check my phone to see?'

Jim Horsley nodded. 'Yes,' he said, for the benefit of the recorder.

Pippa found her call log and scrolled through it. 'Wednesday, 11.03 am. And Janey's call to me last night was at 7.41 pm.'

'Right,' said the policeman, scribbling. 'And why did she call you on Wednesday morning?'

'She wanted me to do a column for the paper, something about crime and past cases. I said no, and told her I'd retired from all that.'

'And how did she take that?'

'She wasn't too happy. I suggested I could write about local event organisation instead, but she turned that idea down flat.'

'Did she seem her normal self in that conversation?'

Pippa thought. 'I think so. She was being nice to get a favour — sort of wheedling me, and when I offered an alternative she made a sharp remark and put the phone down on me.'

Jim Horsley smiled. 'And that was normal?'

Pippa half-smiled back. 'For my relationship with Janey Dixon, such as it was, yes.'

'OK.' The policeman made another note, then looked up. 'We have Ms Dixon's phone and we'll be pulling off the conversations, but that may take time to do.' He paused. 'Why do you think she rang you, given that she'd hung up on you earlier?'

Pippa considered. 'I suppose — I don't mean to sound big-headed but I suppose she thought I could find out who had killed her. I don't think she knew who it was. Her murderer must have thought she was dead, and left. She knew she was dying, so she did the only thing she could think of. She got to her phone somehow, and rang me.'

'And then you drove to the newspaper offices, and identified her.'

'I did.'

The policeman paused. 'This question isn't strictly relevant to the events of last night, but it might be useful. You can answer or not, as you wish. Mrs Parker, did you like Janey Dixon?' His face was neutral in expression.

'Honestly?' Pippa paused as she tried to formulate her answer. 'Not particularly. I respected her, as someone doing her job, but we weren't friends. I only ever spoke to her about things to do with the paper. Never anything personal. If it helps, I don't think she liked me much either. But I think she respected me.'

'Thank you, Mrs Parker, that'll do. Recording ends at eight minutes past ten.' He switched off the recorder, and regarded Pippa. 'Feeling OK?'

Pippa exhaled, and drank some water. 'Yes.' She put her glass down. 'What happens now?'

'Do you have to be anywhere in particular?'

Even as Pippa considered inventing an excuse she found herself saying 'No, not until about one. And I could possibly stretch that a bit.'

'In that case…' Jim Horsley flipped his notebook closed, and shot her a sharp blue glance. 'Inspector Fanshawe and PC Gannet are interviewing the newspaper staff at their offices. The inspector said that if you were free, he'd like me to bring you over. Up for it?'

And this time, Pippa's 'Yes' came without hesitation.

CHAPTER 8

It would have been a ten-minute walk to the newspaper offices from the police station, but PC Horsley took a police car. 'Otherwise people might think I'd arrested you,' he said, grinning.

'I honestly wouldn't be that bothered,' said Pippa. 'People can think what they like.'

'Mm,' said the policeman, starting the engine. 'I don't want people pestering me with questions. *I* do the questions.'

Another police car was parked outside the offices, as well as a Crime Scene Investigation van; presumably Inspector Fanshawe had felt the same way. A receptionist looked up warily as the door opened. 'Can you sign in, please.'

They complied, and were issued with lanyards which said *Gadcester Chronicle — VISITOR*. 'The other two policemen are in the boardroom, on the second floor.' She frowned. 'They said they weren't to be disturbed.'

'Ah. The inspector asked me to bring Mrs Parker over. Could you phone them?'

The receptionist stared at PC Horsley, then, still staring, picked up the receiver and punched in a number. 'It's Diane from reception. You have two visitors, a —' She swivelled the signing-in book towards her. 'PC Horsley, and a Mrs Parker.' A pause. 'I'll let them know.' She replaced the receiver. 'The inspector's waiting for you,' she said, with a hint of accusation that they were still hanging around. 'Straight up to the second floor, and it's the door immediately facing the stairs.'

As they neared the second-floor landing an angry voice floated down to them. 'Don't try to tell me my business!'

Then Inspector Fanshawe's voice, calm and measured. 'I wouldn't dream of it, Mr Tamblyn. However, I'm not sure that mounting a public witch-hunt will do any good.'

Pippa and Jim Horsley exchanged glances. The policeman shrugged, then extended a knuckle and knocked on the glass panel of the boardroom door.

'Come in!' called the inspector.

The two policeman were sitting at the midpoint of a long, polished table, facing the door. Before them were notebooks and a recorder. The man opposite turned to see who had entered. 'You again!' Gerald Tamblyn exclaimed, glaring at Pippa.

'We've finished taking the formal statements,' said the Inspector. 'Mr Tamblyn, may I introduce PC Horsley and Mrs Parker.'

'Ah, so she *does* have a name,' sneered the editor.

'Yes, I do,' said Pippa. 'But I don't like being pressured

to deliver soundbites when someone has just died.'

Inspector Fanshawe raised his eyebrows. 'How interesting. Mr Tamblyn and I have a difference of opinion on the best way of covering the case, media-wise. As you may have heard.'

'The public have a right to know,' said Gerald Tamblyn, loudly.

'Is it in the public interest?' asked the inspector. 'Are the public in danger? I mean, a journalist is killed in her workplace, with a newspaper spike, by someone who presumably works there. It seems a very contained crime to me.'

'None of my team had a reason to kill Janey Dixon.' Gerald Tamblyn put his palms wide apart on the table as if to get up, then kept them there. 'She wasn't well-liked, but that's journalism for you.'

PC Gannet leaned forward, in a manner which suggested he'd seen a policeman do it on TV. 'Off the record, Mr Tamblyn, who do you think killed Janey Dixon?'

The editor looked taken aback, and suddenly seemed much smaller. 'Oh, I can't give an opinion on that sort of thing. I wouldn't want to influence your professional judgement, you see —'

'But off the record?' PC Gannet's eyes had developed a slightly fanatical gleam.

'Could be someone who didn't like what Janey had written about them,' Gerald Tamblyn muttered. 'Or a member of their family. They wait for us by the door sometimes and threaten us. That's why we got the pass

63

system installed.'

'I see,' said PC Gannet, making a note.

'You said that was off the record!' spluttered the editor.

'That wasn't what I was writing down,' said PC Gannet.

'If you've quite finished,' said Gerald Tamblyn, rising, 'I have a newspaper to get out, and a depleted staff to do it with.'

'I'll let you get on,' said Inspector Fanshawe. 'But please, Mr Tamblyn, do stick to the bare facts. Those, and a nice obituary, and an appeal to the public to phone the police station if they saw or heard anything around the offices between six and seven-thirty pm. That's enough for now.'

'Fine,' said the editor. 'Good day to you.' And he stalked out.

Inspector Fanshawe waited until Gerald Tamblyn's footsteps had receded. 'It's been an interesting morning so far.'

'Any leads, sir?' asked PC Horsley.

'I wish,' said the inspector. 'Forensics are nearly done, and they haven't found anything helpful. We've taken statements from the staff based here. That's Mr Tamblyn, Darren Best, chief reporter, Jenny Mace and Graham Dean, both reporters, and Sean Davies, the office junior. They all have alibis for the period of time when Janey Dixon must have been killed. Mr Tamblyn was having dinner with friends, Mr Best was running the pub quiz in his local, Ms Mace was at home with her family, as was Mr Dean, and Mr Davies was playing five-a-side football.'

'So it was someone from outside?'

'It must have been,' said PC Gannet, with a stating-the-obvious air. 'Either someone properly from outside, or someone coming through from the radio station side, seeing as they're based here too.'

'I take it you've checked the door-pass records and the visitors' book,' said Pippa.

PC Gannet gave her a withering look. 'It was one of the first things we did. Everyone's accounted for. No-one signed in who didn't sign out again. Janey Dixon was the last person recorded as being in the building, since the reception closes at six. And before you ask, there were no prints on the spike at all. Whoever did it must have wiped it or worn gloves.'

'Much as it pains me to say it, maybe Gerald Tamblyn's right,' said Pippa. 'Maybe we should get the public on the case. Let's face it, we don't have much to go on.'

Inspector Fanshawe made a face. 'I really don't want to encourage Tamblyn in creating a media storm. Apart from anything else, I don't think he's got the resources to do it.'

'That's a good point,' said Pippa. 'I thought a lot more people wrote for the *Chronicle* than that. What about Harry Poynter who does the theatre reviews, or Susan James who does the movies? Who does the sports?'

'The people I've named, plus Janey,' said Inspector Fanshawe. 'I asked about all the missing bylines and apparently they were shared out among the remaining staff some time ago. Downsizing, you see. Janey did films, theatre, horoscopes, the agony column, the society pages…'

'Gosh,' said Pippa. 'No wonder she was after me for

more content.'

'Mmm.' Inspector Fanshawe lined up his notebook and pen. 'It was also one of the reasons why she wasn't particularly well-liked. Darren Best said that Janey poached stories from him more than once. Jenny Mace said that she was always breathing down her neck, trying to muscle in. And Gerald Tamblyn confirmed that Janey had asked him to reassign other people's work to her, on the quiet.'

'Oh dear.'

'Yes. But now there'll be more than enough work to go round.'

When professionalism goes into overdrive, thought Pippa, and Suze floated into her mind. *I must text later and explain.* 'Have you found a contact for Janey, or a next of kin, or anything?'

'Eventually,' said PC Gannet. 'Tamblyn dug in the files. There's a former partner, and that's it. No parents or siblings or children.'

'How strange,' said Pippa. 'I mean, not to update that after you break up with someone.'

'I don't think there was anyone to update it with,' said the Inspector. 'Janey Dixon appears to have been very much a loner. Married to her work, you could say. Anyway, he's been informed. He was — surprised, and then again not. But apparently there isn't any other family. He told me that Janey grew up in a children's home.'

'Oh gosh, how sad.' Pippa tried to imagine a young, sharp-faced Janey, and found it surprisingly easy.

'It is, rather,' said the inspector. 'But there's nothing we can do about it.' He sighed and stretched his legs under the table. 'OK, what do we do now?'

'We could go and interview her ex-partner,' said PC Gannet.

'They broke up years ago,' said the Inspector. 'But yes, we could.'

'We could get the radio station people in,' said PC Horsley. 'One of them might have seen something. Perhaps one of the newspaper staff confided in them. That sort of thing happens.'

'True,' said the inspector.

'Could we —' Everyone turned to look at Pippa. 'Could we get a list of all the ins and outs from the building?'

'We already checked that,' said PC Gannet, shifting in his chair.

'I'm sure you have. But maybe analyse the whole week. That way we could get a sense of people's routines, including Janey's. And someone could talk to Diane on reception. She'd probably be able to tell you all sorts.'

PC Gannet snorted. 'About her false nails or celebrity gossip, maybe.'

'That's a good point,' said Jim Horsley. 'Pippa, if we can get that list, would you mind checking it?'

'Sure,' said Pippa. 'That's something I can do at home. And speaking of home, I'd better go and pick Ruby up before she wears out her welcome.'

The inspector smiled. 'Oh yes, how is Miss Bump?'

Pippa grinned, remembering her first encounters with Inspector Fanshawe, when Ruby had indeed been a bump. 'Feisty. Not much gets past her.'

'Takes after mum then,' said Jim Horsley. 'I can run you back to the station if you like.'

'That's fine, I'll walk.' Pippa glanced at her phone. One voicemail. She blinked and put the phone in her bag. That could keep until she was on her own in the car. She had a feeling that whatever it was would be swear-worthy. 'Let me know what happens.'

'We shall,' said the inspector. He sighed. 'This seems far more complicated than it ought to be.'

Pippa went downstairs, signed out, and handed her badge back to Diane, who was flicking through a copy of *Take a Break*. 'It's a terrible shame, isn't it,' she said.

'It was. I've told the management they shouldn't let people work late, but do they listen? And now look!' Diane breathed hard and glared at the street. 'Poor woman.' Her expression softened a little. 'I liked her, you know. No nonsense about her. "Morning Diane," she'd say, and be on her way. None of this *could you just*, or *would you mind*, or whining about a parcel that hadn't been delivered or a room they wanted booking or a taxi to go to the other side of town or a parking pass for a friend.' She took a breath. 'She got on with her job. Barely saw her, to be honest. Half the time she was here before me and still at her desk when I left.'

'I see,' said Pippa.

'Anyway,' said Diane, refocusing on her, 'I'm sure you have places to be.'

'I do indeed,' said Pippa, and left.

The pale autumn sun on her face was pleasant. She walked back to the police station, got into the Mini, braced herself, and pressed *Play* on her voicemail.

'Hello, this is Suze. I have no idea why you're blanking me like this. I thought we were friends.' A pause. 'My client is disposed to go ahead. Please call back ASAP.'

Pippa threw the phone onto the passenger seat and started the engine. *Not now, Suze*, she thought, manoeuvring the Mini out of its space and towards the exit. *At this rate, perhaps not ever.*

CHAPTER 9

'Plans for today?' asked Simon, as he put his tie on.

Pippa pulled the quilt down enough to see him. 'Wake up. Get Freddie to school. Caitlin's Josh is coming for a playdate this morning, and then we're meeting at the tearoom for the cake she says I owe her.'

'Work sounds quite nice now.' Simon eased his tie up, gazed in the mirror and fiddled with it. When he'd finished it looked exactly the same.

'You're bright and early. And why the tie, on a Friday?'

'Meeting.'

'Ohhh. Is it the sort of meeting that'll make you late home?'

'Hope not. But you probably shouldn't cook a three-course masterpiece.'

Pippa snorted. 'I'm not sure I ever have.'

Simon leaned down for a kiss, his tie draping over the duvet. 'And will you speak to Suze?'

Pippa pulled the duvet over her head. 'Aaargh.'

'Come on, what's the worst that could happen?'

'She could steamroller me and Serendipity into something. Or I could be so rude to her that she never speaks to me again.'

'Ah.' Simon straightened up. 'I guess that's a no, then.' He headed to the door and paused, hand on the doorknob. 'Are you likely to be doing any police work?'

'I doubt it,' said Pippa. 'There isn't much I can do, not with Ruby in tow.' She emerged from the covers and reached for her cooling mug of tea. 'If there is, I'm sure Piglet will let me know.'

Simon grinned. 'Does he know you call him Piglet?'

'I don't, it's his phone book entry. And no, he doesn't.'

'That's as well. You might be arrested for insulting a police officer. And on that note, I'll see you later.'

Pippa blew him a kiss and finished her tea. She should really get up and mobilise the children, but the bed was so lovely and warm... She picked up her phone and typed *Gadcester Chronicle* into her search engine.

The homepage now had a black border. *TRAGIC DEATH OF STAR JOURNALIST.* Underneath was a short article.

Janey Dixon, well-loved reporter at the Gadcester Chronicle, was found dead at the Chronicle offices on Wednesday evening. We are all devastated, and we are working with the police to bring Janey's killer to justice.

As a result, your newspaper will be a little slimmer today, and possibly for the next few days. Please bear with us at this difficult time.

Below was a link to Janey Dixon's obituary. Pippa clicked, and read.

Janey Dixon, who has died at the age of 52, was a well-known journalist in the Gadcestershire area. However, she was perhaps a less well-known face. Janey was a private person, and though there were opportunities for her to appear at public events, Janey rarely took these up. Journalism was her life.

Janey grew up in Derbyshire, and after studying journalism at college she started work at a local paper. There she quickly rose from office junior to cub reporter, and also began writing the opinion pieces for which she is best known.

Janey moved to the Gadcester Chronicle in 2001, quickly becoming an indispensable part of the team. Until her death, she was the longest-serving current member of staff.

Janey will be remembered for her energy, stamina, and passion for journalism. She will be sadly missed by her colleagues and, we are sure, by the community in Gadcestershire.

'Nice job,' Pippa commented. She scrolled down and noted that comments were turned off. Clearly Gerald Tamblyn wasn't risking the community in Gadcestershire leaving their thoughts about Janey Dixon.

Right. Up. Children. Breakfast.

'I'm gonna make a rocket, I'm gonna make a rocket!' sang Freddie, as she buttered his toast.

'Indeed you are,' said Pippa. 'And it's "going to", not "gonna".'

'*MegaMoose* says gonna,' said Freddie. 'And he's a superhero.'

'I bet Miss Darcy doesn't say gonna,' replied Pippa.

She'd caught him on his weak point. Freddie adored Miss Darcy, to the point where he occasionally addressed Pippa as such. Freddie muttered 'going to', and accepted his toast.

'What we doing, Mummy?' asked Ruby.

'Playdate,' said Pippa. 'Josh is coming round this morning, and then there will be cake.'

Ruby's eyes were round as chocolate buttons. 'Making cake?'

'No, tearoom cake,' said Pippa.

'Ohh.' Ruby pouted. 'Josh's mum makes cake. Nice cake.'

'Does she now,' said Pippa, resolving that she would have a word with Caitlin when Ruby wasn't listening. 'Well, I'm sure tearoom cake will be much nicer than any cake Mummy could make.'

Ruby considered, toast waving in the air. 'Yes,' she said, and, the matter settled to her satisfaction, ate half her slice in one bite.

***

Pippa arrived home from the tearoom wanting nothing so much as a nap. After a panini and a large slice of carrot cake, she felt as if she had swallowed a lead weight. 'The carbs, the carbs,' she muttered.

'What, Mummy?' asked Ruby, who had followed her

brother's tradition of demanding beans on toast, and whose eyelids were drooping.

'Nothing, Ruby,' said Pippa. 'Just Mummy being silly.'

Her phone rang and she pulled it out of her pocket, with difficulty. The display said *Serendipity*.

Pippa stared at it. 'Serendipity hardly ever rings me,' she said. 'She texts.'

'Sippidippy run away again?' asked Ruby, her face disapproving.

'I think I need to find out,' said Pippa, and hit *Answer*.

'I'm so sorry to phone, Pippa, but I don't know what to do,' gabbled Serendipity.

Pippa frowned. 'Aren't you supposed to be in Gadding Magna for your demo?'

'*She's* here again.'

'Your mother?'

'Yes. And she's parked right across River Lane. I'm trapped.' A nervous giggle. 'I'm actually trapped.'

'She can't do that,' said Pippa.

'Well, she has.'

'Right. I think I can sort this. Give me a few minutes. Wait — when does your demo start?'

'Half past two,' said Serendipity. 'I can still do it. I packed the car earlier. But —'

'I'll do my best,' said Pippa, and ended the call. She scrolled through her contacts.

'How odd,' said Jim Horsley. 'I was about to ring you.'

'Were you?'

'I was. The pass system info has just come in. Want me to print it and drop it off? I'm in the village today.'

'Yes please. But I need you to do something a bit more local first.'

'Oh yes?'

'Yes. I have to report an obstruction.'

***

Jim Horsley rang back twenty minutes later. 'All done, madam.'

'And Serendipity's managed to get out?'

He tutted. 'Obviously. I'm not sure pulling me off a murder investigation to get your friend to her craft demo is entirely legitimate.'

'It was a legitimate obstruction though.'

He was silent.

Pippa's heart sank. 'It was, wasn't it?' *Don't tell me Serendipity's flipped from stress.*

'I might have to pay a call and deliver a caution.' PC Horsley's voice had developed a stern edge.

Pippa swallowed. 'Might you?'

'Yes. To be very careful with the information I'm about to deliver.'

'You rotten —'

'See you soon.'

***

'So what happened?' asked Pippa, opening the door.

'I believe "Good morning officer, would you like a cuppa?" is the usual greeting,' observed PC Horsley, stepping inside. 'What have you done with Ruby?'

'Put her down for a nap,' said Pippa. 'She's had a big lunch and needs a sleep. As do I.'

Jim Horsley raised his eyebrows.

'However, as you're here I shall put the kettle on.' Pippa walked through to the kitchen, hoping that she wasn't blushing.

'So, Mrs Parker,' said PC Horsley, following her, 'I proceeded to River Lane in my police car and found the situation much as it had been described by a concerned member of the public. That's you, by the way.'

Pippa got mugs from the cupboard. 'And?'

'A large black Range Rover was parked across the entrance to River Lane, and a woman dressed for — I'm not sure what, but not a country walk — was standing outside Ms Jones's house.'

'Go on.' Pippa dropped teabags into the mugs and leaned on the worktop.

'I gave my siren a couple of peals and she stood to attention. I wound down the window and explained that she was causing an obstruction and I would like her to clear it. Then I drove past the entrance to River Lane and waited. And waited some more. When I got out my notebook and began writing in it, she came over.'

'Were you taking the car details?' asked Pippa.

'I was making a shopping list. However, she didn't know that. "Is there a problem, officer?" she asked, as if butter wouldn't melt. I replied that yes, her car was the problem and I needed it out of the way as it was blocking access.'

'Ooooooo,' said Pippa.

'Then she said she wasn't on any yellow lines, and I said that if she wanted I could look up parking regulations and give her a breakdown of exactly what I would charge

76

her with. "Do you have a reason to be here, madam?" I asked, and she said she had been visiting a friend. So I said that I would see her on her way. She got into the vehicle, executed a thirteen-point turn or thereabouts, and proceeded into the main road, where the vehicle stopped. The main road does have yellow lines, so I pulled in behind her, put on the blue lights, and escorted her all the way to Lower Gadding.'

'You hero!' exclaimed Pippa, and gave him a one-armed hug before she had quite realised.

'Well, um,' said Jim Horsley, and stared at his feet.

'I'll make that tea,' she gabbled. 'Did you bring the door data?'

'I did,' he said, taking off his hat and scratching his head. 'It's in the car, I'll go and get it.'

Pippa put her hands to her cheeks. Then she texted Serendipity. *Did you get out OK?* She waited, then remembered Serendipity was probably driving. *Fair enough.*

The policeman came back in with a buff envelope. 'Here you go,' he said. 'It's fairly straightforward, but you'll need a key for the passcodes. Keep it to yourself, and that's an order. This isn't the sort of thing we'd normally hand out. Gannet was scandalised.'

'Good,' said Pippa. Her phone buzzed.

Serendipity: *Made it! Just setting up, then I'll ring.*

'She made it,' said Pippa, showing Jim her message. 'Good work, officer.'

Jim Horsley snorted. 'Indeed.' He pulled the transcript from its envelope. 'I suggest you make that tea before it's stewed, and then we can go through this properly.'

'Yes sir.' Pippa flicked the teabags into the bin and went to the fridge for milk. Her phone sang out, and she picked it up. 'Well done!' she cried.

'I was about to say the same to you,' said Suze. 'Or rather, not.'

Pippa debated on whether to end the call right there, but she was in the mood to vent her anger. 'I assume that little exhibition was your idea.'

'It might have been,' said Suze. 'I certainly didn't expect you to send the local bobby to do your dirty work, though.' A pause. 'Friend of yours, is he?'

Pippa *knew* her cheeks were burning now. 'He was doing his job. Your client was causing an obstruction.'

'All she wants to do is talk to her daughter,' said Suze, very reasonably.

'Well, her daughter doesn't want to talk to her,' snapped Pippa. 'Now if you've finished, I'm waiting for a call.'

'I'll let you get on, then,' said Suze. 'Just one final thing. If you're going to play dirty tricks, so am I. It's all-out war, Pippa, as far as I'm concerned. You can wave a white flag, or you can engage and accept the consequences. And I don't think you'll like them. Ciao.'

And the phone went dead.

Pippa's arm went back to throw the phone at the wall, but her wrist was caught and the phone gently removed. 'That's a nice handset,' said Jim, mildly. 'And it isn't the phone's fault.'

'I know,' said Pippa, and sighed.

'Are you all right?' he asked. His hand was still holding her wrist, encircling it easily. It was a large hand, with square-tipped fingers, the nails neatly trimmed. 'You don't look all right.'

'That, believe it or not, was a friend,' said Pippa. 'Only now she's a rival. And I've got what — who — she wants.'

'Serendipity?' asked Jim.

Pippa nodded.

Slowly, he let go. Pippa half-wished he wouldn't. 'You sit down, and I'll do the tea.'

Pippa walked into the dining room. Her head was buzzing and everything sounded louder than normal. *How on earth have things come to this*?

Jim Horsley came through with a tray, on which were two mugs and a packet of chocolate Hobnobs. 'I hope you weren't saving these for anything special,' he said.

Pippa's mouth wobbled, and she put her hands to her face. The tray thunked down, and a moment later she felt an arm round her, and leaned her head on a comforting, warm woollen jumper. 'I'll be all right — in a moment — really I will,' she gasped, between sobs.

'Shhh,' he replied, his breath ruffling her hair. 'Shhh.'

CHAPTER 10

Gently, Pippa disengaged herself. 'Sorry,' she muttered. 'Too many things at once.' Her eyes were swollen, and she suspected she looked a complete fright.

'No need to apologise,' said Jim Horsley, passing her a mug of tea and putting the biscuits between them.

Pippa sipped from her steaming mug, and felt better. It helped that PC Horsley didn't seem remotely embarrassed by what had happened. Then again, maybe rural policemen did comforting as part of the job. Telling old ladies their cat had been run over. Picking up lost children and taking them home. That sort of thing. 'We'd better go through these passcodes before Ruby wakes up,' she said.

'Yes, we had.' Jim Horsley opened his notebook. In it was a handwritten list of numbers, and next to it, the corresponding names of staff from the newspaper and the radio station. 'I haven't had time to re-copy this,' he said. 'Please use initials, for security.'

Pippa fetched her own notebook and did as she was

told. The act of writing was soothing. PC Horsley's handwriting was bold, the capitals blocky. He probably had to write legibly as part of his job. Like primary-school teachers.

'Do you need anything else?' asked the policeman.

Pippa shook her head.

'I'll leave you to it, then.' He drained his mug and set it on the tray, then looked at her. 'You might want to wash your face before Ruby wakes.'

'Is it that bad?'

'No, not at all, but —'

'Hint taken.' She sighed. 'Thanks for — you know.'

'Think nothing of it,' the policeman replied.

She saw him to the door. 'If I find anything, I'll phone.'

'I know you will.' He put on his hat. 'Good luck, Pippa.'

She closed the door quietly, and listened for the sound of a car engine, which did not come. He was probably picking up messages, working out where to head to next.

In the mirror over the sink her face was blotchy and a bit unfocused, as if someone had taken a brush and blurred her at the edges. *Ugh.* Pippa dried herself, returned to the dining room, and found a pencil.

Putting initials next to each door code was easy enough. It was a long list, covering the week up to Janey's murder and the week before. Pippa worked through the list methodically, then sat back and considered it.

Some people's code appeared much more frequently in the printout. Gerald Tamblyn, for example, came in at half past nine on most days, then out for ten, back in for half eleven, and then out again between half past twelve and two, before leaving at half past five. In contrast, Sean Davies was usually in at five past nine, out from twelve till one, and left for the day at five to five.

Now, what about Janey?

'Mummy?'

Pippa stiffened.

'Mummy, can I get up now?'

Pippa put the printed sheets and her notepad in the drawer and closed it. 'Yes, Ruby, I'm coming up.'

Ruby looked as bright as a button when Pippa went upstairs. 'Is it time to go to school?'

Pippa checked her watch. 'Good grief, it almost is. But let's check that nappy first.'

After school was taken up with Freddie's rocket, a glorious affair of silver foil with stuck-on windows, and tissue-paper flames issuing from its rear. Freddie charged around the village green making rocket noises, to the consternation of the ducks. Then he halted, mid-flight. 'What's the time?' he asked.

'A quarter to four,' said Pippa. 'Three forty-five,' she clarified.

'*MegaMoose* has started!' he cried, his face full of woe.

'Never mind,' said Pippa. 'We can probably find it on catch-up.' But Freddie was unconsoled, and his rocket flew no more.

'It's only a TV show, Freddie,' said Pippa.

Freddie shrugged. 'What if I never see it?'

'That's pretty unlikely. Let's go home and see if we can track it down.'

They got back in time to catch the closing credits, and despite fifteen minutes of searching in the farthest reaches of the channel guide and catch-up TV, Pippa's quest was fruitless. 'I'll set it to record the series next time it's on,' she said. 'That way this won't happen again.'

'But it already happened,' said Freddie, and went up to his room.

What a day, thought Pippa, and went to make a cup of tea. Jim Horsley's mug was still in the sink, and she washed it and put it away while the kettle boiled. Not that she wouldn't tell Simon he had called in . . . but the kitchen looked better tidy.

When Simon got home just after seven he was full of his meeting, and the various options for how things might work. That took them through cooking, eating, and loading the dishwasher.

'And what about you?' he asked, as he dropped the cutlery into the basket. 'How was your day?'

'Grisly,' said Pippa. 'Ruby had a playdate this morning, Suze is out for blood and Freddie missed *MegaMoose.*'

Simon looked contrite. 'Sorry I didn't ask before.'

'S'OK,' said Pippa. 'Let's go and shout at the television.'

***

'Pippa.'

Pippa started guiltily. Simon, in his dressing gown, was framed in the dining-room doorway.

'It's half six in the morning. And it's Saturday.'

'I know. I couldn't sleep.'

'Is it the Suze thing?'

She sighed. 'Partly. But Janey's on my mind too.'

'Of course she will be.' He came over and kissed the top of her head. 'But sitting up staring at papers probably won't help. You need sleep.'

'I was wide awake. There's no point tossing and turning and waking you up as well.'

Simon peered at the papers. 'What is all that, anyway?'

'Door-pass codes, from the police,' said Pippa. 'I'm trying to find a pattern.'

Simon blinked. 'And have you?'

'Not yet. Except that Janey Dixon was pretty much glued to her desk. Or certainly the building.'

'I'll leave you to it.' Simon yawned. 'If you're still down here at half seven, bring me up some tea.'

'Yes, boss,' said Pippa, and bent her head to her work again.

Janey had been a hard worker. In most days before eight, and often still there at seven, without going out for lunch. Pippa imagined her at her desk, eating — what? Not a homemade packed lunch. Maybe a sandwich she'd picked up on the way in, or perhaps she lived on black coffee and adrenaline. She had even gone in last Saturday morning for three hours.

Pippa followed Janey's initials through the week leading to her death. Strange, she hadn't signed out on the Monday, and there was nothing for Tuesday, or Wednesday morning. And then, of course, the killer had signed themselves out with her pass that evening, at 7.02 pm.

Perhaps she'd actually taken a day off. She deserved it.

But who would take a day off on a Tuesday, unless they

84

had an appointment? And why hadn't Janey signed out on Monday, or in on Wednesday? She was normally as regular as clockwork.

Pippa wrote in her notebook. *Find out if Janey took a day off on Tuesday, and whether she had a meeting outside the office on Monday afternoon.*

Perhaps she had followed someone out of the building on Monday. That way she wouldn't have needed to use her pass. Or she could have left with them.

Pippa scribbled more notes, then pushed her hair back from her face. This made everything more complicated. For all they knew, the staff could have been going in and out together at any time, and only one pass would have been logged by the system. Or someone going out could have held the door for someone going in —

'This is getting like Fox and Geese,' she said, aloud. 'Why did I volunteer for this?'

After another ten minutes of drawing lines and writing notes, she looked at the clock. Quarter-past seven. *Brain officially fried.* She put the printouts in the drawer and went to make tea.

The radio was playing quietly when she took the drinks upstairs. 'This isn't the usual power pop I expect on a Saturday morning,' she said, handing Simon his mug. 'Have you changed stations?'

'Nope,' said Simon. 'I think Ritz is on holiday.'

'Oh.' Pippa got back into bed.

'Any progress on cracking the Da Vinci Code?'

'Nope,' said Pippa. 'It's getting worse, not better.'

'Oh dear.'

'Missing You' came on. 'Good grief,' said Pippa. 'If this doesn't improve I might switch over.'

'A bit of Chris de Burgh there for you. Um, this is Tony Jeffries in for Ritz Robertson on the Saturday Ritz Show, and that song is also for Ritz, who sadly can't do the show today. Sending you all the best, Ritz, and hoping you're back with us soon.' A pause. 'And here's Kylie and Jason.'

'That's odd,' said Pippa, as 'Especially for You' kicked in. 'Have you ever known Ritz Robertson be off air? I mean apart from holidays.'

'Not that I'm a dedicated Gadcester FM listener, but no,' said Simon. 'I bet he'd broadcast from his hospital bed if he had to.'

'Mmm,' said Pippa, and reached for her phone. *Ritz Robertson isn't doing his show*, she texted. *Is he OK?*

She pressed *Send. Was that the right thing to do?*, she thought. Texting a police officer, at this time on a Saturday?

Then again, if something had happened to Ritz…

A reply flashed up. *I'll check.*

'Who are you texting?' asked Simon.

'Jim Horsley, in case he knows anything.'

Simon frowned. 'Why would a Much Gadding policeman know anything about a Gadcester DJ?'

'I'm not going to text Inspector Fanshawe at this time, am I?' Pippa opened her browser and typed *Ritz Robertson*. The results brought nothing useful back, and she sighed.

'We're getting listener requests in, and here's a tune to cheer you up, Ritz, if you're listening. Elaine from Lower

Gadding has requested 'Walking on Sunshine' because that's how your show makes her feel.' Tony Jeffries sounded rather disgusted. 'Take it away, Katrina and her Waves!'

Pippa's phone buzzed.

Piglet: *Checked in with main station. Ritz taken to hospital after crash just outside Gadcester this morning. Minor injuries they think but keeping him in. No other driver involved.*

Pippa stared at the phone. 'Oh no.'

'What now?' said Simon.

'Ritz Robertson's been in a car crash. Minor though.'

'That isn't too bad.' Simon drank some tea. 'Hopefully he'll be back soon and this guy can go back to the midnight shift or whatever it is he does.' He looked at Pippa over his mug. 'Pippa, these things happen. You can't assume that everything is linked to Janey Dixon's murder.'

Pippa's phone flashed again. *Good call by the way. Jim.*

'Mmm,' said Pippa. 'We'll see.'

CHAPTER 11

Simon made a point of keeping the family busy all day. A cooked breakfast, then the big shop, followed by drinks and cake in the cafe, and then off to the local mini farm and petting zoo.

'Is this to take my mind off things?' asked Pippa, while the children were stroking a donkey's nose.

'Yes,' Simon replied. 'Ritz was probably speeding, or something. And if there is anything dodgy about it, there isn't much you can do to find out. Leave it to the police, do.'

'I am doing!' cried Pippa, and the donkey looked over.

'*Mummy!*' the children whined. 'You scared Dapple!'

'Now then,' said Simon. 'No donkey cruelty.'

'Oh do shut up.' But Pippa giggled. Maybe she *was* jumping to conclusions.

They had lunch in the farm restaurant, and Pippa tried not to reflect that she could probably have prepared the same things more quickly and for a fraction of the cost.

The children were hoovering up their food happily, and that was what counted.

'What will you do about Suze?' asked Simon.

Pippa shrugged. 'I have no idea. Warn Serendipity, definitely.'

Simon looked up from his ploughman's lunch. 'You mean you haven't already?'

'She was so happy,' said Pippa, miserably. 'I couldn't burst her bubble.'

Serendipity had sent her various photos from the craft demonstration: a row of pastel-painted bird-boxes, several pictures of smiling women holding paintbrushes, and a shot of a flowered plate being used as a palette. *We could use these on the website*, she had texted. *Everyone signed up for the full workshop. Thank you so much for your help. Hopefully Mummy has got the message.*

Hopefully, Pippa had texted back. Mummy might have got the message, but Suze had taken it as a shot across her bows.

'I will speak to her,' she said. 'But not today.'

After lunch there were ducks and geese, and a pair of pot-bellied pigs which fascinated Freddie. Pippa was taking a picture of him scratching behind Spot's ears when the phone buzzed. She took the shot, then looked.

Insp F: *Gannet visited Ritz in hospital. Whiplash, cuts and bruises but stable. Adamant he wasn't speeding but says it happened so fast he's not sure how.*

Pippa laughed. 'Seems you were right.'

She showed the text to Simon, who put an arm round her. 'Told you so, worryguts.' They leaned on the fence, watching the children. 'Those two will need a bath later.'

'Their clothes will probably need fumigating. The farmyard smell is strong with this one,' Pippa said, pointing at Spot.

'Bit harsh,' said Simon, kissing Pippa.

At home Simon supervised bath time while Pippa put a wash on and started a sauce for lasagne. She was going to make it from scratch; no bottles, no jars, no packets — apart from ready-done pasta sheets, she wasn't mad. Today had been lovely, and her fears were unfounded. She should stop over-analysing.

Pippa chopped garlic and onions and slid them into the frying pan, then went to the fridge for mince. Her phone buzzed on the worktop.

Piglet: *You won't believe this.*

Pippa put the pack of mince down. *I won't believe what?,* she replied.

Report from the garage. Ritz's brakes were tampered with.

Pippa's hand began to shake.

A specialist team went over the car. They found something in the glove compartment. A badge, with the letter B. Gannet showed it to Ritz, and he says it isn't his. Never seen it before.

***

Pippa turned the pan off and dashed into the lounge. Her Agatha Christie collection was on the second shelf down, a group of battered paperbacks picked up from charity shops. Did she have the one she needed?

No.

Unless it was in her reading pile upstairs… She ran into the bedroom, scooped up the pile of books on the floor and dumped them on the bed. *Eleanor Oliphant . . . Trouble with Goats and Sheep . . . Crooked House…*

'Are you all right?' called Simon. 'Come on, Freddie, time to get out.'

'Just looking for something.' Pippa checked Simon's stack of books. Not there either. 'Would you mind if I popped into the village? I'll only be a few minutes.' Without waiting for an answer, she ran downstairs and grabbed her keys.

It was a quarter to five, and the village was showing signs of closing for the day. The grocer was taking in the boxes of veg stacked outside, and the lights were out in Polly's Whatnots. Pippa ran past the tearoom and flung herself at the door of the library. It opened easily and she stumbled over the threshold.

'That was quite an entrance,' said Norm, as Pippa came to rest against a revolving leaflet stand. 'On a mission, are we?'

'Yes,' said Pippa, righting herself. '*The ABC Murders*. Do you have it? Actually, yes, I'm sure you do.' She hurried to the crime shelves and found *C*.

Again, everything *but The ABC Murders* was there. But if someone had taken it out…

She pushed her fringe out of her eyes and walked to the desk. 'Could you look it up, please?' she said.

Norm raised his eyebrows. 'I could.' He put down the

book he was reading — a Douglas Reeman — selected a ledger from his small stack, and leafed through the pages, working back from the last entry. Pippa tried not to twitch at the slow deliberation of his movements.

Norman glanced up. 'Can I ask why you want to know?'

Pippa checked the library was otherwise empty, and considered how much she could tell him. He was an ex-policeman, after all. 'I think there's a link between Ritz Robertson's accident and Janey Dixon's murder, and *The ABC Murders* might help. If someone's taken it out, and they could have been involved...' Her voice faltered under his steady gaze.

'I see,' he said. 'You may want to reconsider that.' He laid his book over the following entries, then turned the ledger to face her.

At the top of the page was written *8th August, ABC Murders — Pippa Parker.*

'But I haven't got it,' said Pippa.

'The ledger says you have,' said Norm. 'And that looks like my writing. Now I can't remember issuing it to you, but it isn't unlikely that you would have borrowed it. You're my best crime customer, and you specialise in the Golden Age.'

'True,' said Pippa. 'But I don't remember borrowing it, either.'

'It's probably at the bottom of a bag somewhere,' said Norm. 'The kids distracted you or the phone rang, and you never got round to taking it out. That's the sort of thing that happens to me.'

'I suppose,' said Pippa.

'Maybe you're getting to that age,' said Norm.

'Do you mind, I'm thirty-one!' cried Pippa, and then saw Norm's sly grin. 'Very funny. Fine, I'll go and hunt it out.'

'You do that,' said Norm, closing the ledger. 'Now if you don't mind, it's time to shut up shop. I doubt I'll have any more eager readers battering my door down with questions.'

Pippa giggled. 'Sorry about that. And I'd better go. If I don't get on with dinner, the children might eat Simon.'

'Ah, the ravenous age,' said Norm. 'They'll get over that in fifteen years or so.'

Pippa returned home at a much more sedate speed than she had set out. The village was looking very pretty, with the dying sun sprinkling glitter on the duck pond, the sky putting on a show of indigo and orange, and lights twinkling on the other side of the green, but Pippa saw none of it. She was wrapped up in trying to remember what she had been doing on the day she had allegedly borrowed the book. And in trying to recall the plot. She had read it, she *knew* she had, but it had been a while, and it was easy to get one's Agathas mixed up... She pulled out her key and opened the door. Strains of cartoon music wafted from the lounge.

Simon walked into the hall. 'Care to explain where you've been?' He was wearing an apron and wielding a wooden spoon. *Oh dear.*

'I needed to get to the library before it closed,' said Pippa. 'Sorry. But I've only been out a few minutes.'

'Couldn't it have waited?' Simon folded his arms, despite the spoon.

'Not if I wanted to get there before Monday —'

'That's what I mean,' said Simon. 'I tried to make sure we all had a nice day together as a family to take your mind off the Ritz thing, and the minute we get home you go dashing off again in response to a text from your friend Jim.'

Pippa recalled her phone, sitting on the worktop, and blinked. 'Colleague. That's why I went to the library. Something isn't right.'

'There's always something.' Simon's face was as grim and stern as if it were cut from stone.

'What do you mean?'

'I don't know,' he said, and his bottom lip wobbled a fraction. 'But I'd rather you spent less time texting Jim Horsley.'

'It was about work!'

'It isn't your work. It's police work. You're neglecting your own work to help them.'

Conflicting thoughts rushed through Pippa's brain —

He's right...

But it is my work, sort of...

My contact with Jim Horsley is entirely work-related...

And you need to make sure it stays that way...

'It's a mess,' she said finally, tucking her hair behind her ears as if that would tidy it. 'The whole thing's a mess. But I do think I'm on to something. When we've got the kids to bed I can tell you about it, if you want.'

Simon's shoulders relaxed. 'That would be — well, not

nice, but I'd appreciate it. Sometimes I feel out of the loop, as Declan would say. And when I saw that text —' He pushed his hair back. 'Sandy next door had a joke with me as I was coming in yesterday evening. She said the police had been round that afternoon to arrest you.'

'Oh yes, PC Horsley dropped off the door-pass data.'

'I bet he did.' Simon seemed to look everywhere but at her. 'It's not that I don't trust you, Pippa, but maybe next time you could go to the station…'

Pippa considered making a case involving Ruby's nap, but it seemed like too much trouble. 'OK. Got the message. Now, do you want me to take over the lasagne?'

Simon smiled, but it was the kind of smile that could vanish very easily. 'If you like. Or you can come and help me.'

'Aye aye, Cap'n.' Pippa put aside thoughts of finding plot summaries on Wikipedia, or texting Jim Horsley back, and followed Simon into the kitchen.

CHAPTER 12

'So,' said Simon. 'Tell me about this case.'

The children had been put to bed twenty minutes ago, and so far there had been no cries of 'Mummy, I'm thirsty!', or 'Rupert fell out of bed!'

Pippa got up from the sofa, went to the door and listened. 'I think we're safe.' She looked round at Simon. 'Do you want coffee?'

'Yeah, go on,' said Simon. 'That feels more detective-y than tea.'

'Huh,' said Pippa. 'The police force runs on tea, you know.'

She had left her phone in the kitchen to avoid temptation, and now it was staring at her. 'Stop it,' she said, and turned it over. When she came back into the lounge Simon had muted the television, and was sitting up expectantly. 'Gimme the lowdown,' he growled. 'I need a big desk and a swivel chair.'

Pippa snorted. 'We could go in the dining room if you'd

96

prefer.'

They sat facing each other, mugs on coasters. 'Where do you want me to start?' asked Pippa.

'Wherever you like,' said Simon. 'It's rather exciting.'

'It's also confidential,' warned Pippa.

Simon rolled his eyes. 'Don't worry, I'm not planning to do story time at work.'

'OK.' And Pippa outlined events so far. Simon's eyes widened as she spoke.

'Wow.' He sat back and put his arms behind his head. 'And you think this book has something to do with it.' He thought. 'Wasn't it on TV a while ago?'

'It was,' said Pippa, 'but I stopped watching. It got — weird.'

'Oh, one of *those* adaptations,' said Simon. 'Speaking of which, I watched a bit of *MegaMoose* with Freddie earlier. He's like Inspector Gadget, but a moose.'

'That makes sense,' said Pippa. 'Unlike Norm's ledger. I'm *sure* I haven't borrowed that book. I mean, I'd remember.'

'You would,' said Simon. 'You forget lots of things, but when it comes to books, you're on it.' He sipped his black coffee, made a face, and put the mug down. 'So what do you think happened?'

'The book wasn't in the library — or at least, not where it should have been. Norm's very meticulous, so the book must be out.' Pippa visualised the layout of the library. 'The crime shelves are near the door, at the opposite end of the library to Norm's desk. It would be easy for someone to take a book from there, and there aren't any alarms.'

'OK, but what about the ledger?'

'It looked like Norm's handwriting,' said Pippa, beginning to doubt herself. 'Not that I could see the rest of the page; he put a book over it. The entry was right at the top.'

Simon sipped his coffee again, carefully. 'When you say right at the top...'

'Yes. In fact...' Pippa's eyebrows knitted as she tried to remember the page. 'It wasn't written on a line. It was above the line.'

'So it could have been squished in afterwards!' Simon set his mug down with a clack. 'Someone could have pinched the book, then at any time caused a distraction to get Norm out of the way, and popped your details in a blank space in the ledger.'

'Go to the top of the class.' Pippa reached across to shake Simon's hand. 'But why?'

Simon counted the reasons on his fingers. 'Either they want to get you banned from the library, or they want people to think you have the book, or they're telling you that they're on to you, or...'

'Or...?' Pippa felt genuinely puzzled.

'Or . . . they want to frame you.' The words came slowly, and Simon's face changed as he said them. He got up. 'Is your phone still in the kitchen?'

'It is.' Pippa felt as if she were in a dream, and not a good one. 'What do you want it for?'

'If you don't mind, I'm going to ring Jim Horsley. I'm not having people implicating you in this.'

'So killing people is all right, but not faking library

records?'

'You know what I mean.'

'Can we at least get our facts straight?' Pippa got up and took her laptop from its bag. 'I could be completely misremembering the book. And the library thing could be an honest mistake. Maybe the person who's got *The ABC Murders* has one of my books written against their name. Human error.'

'Maybe.' But Simon didn't sound convinced.

'Here's the plot, anyway.' Simon came to sit beside her, and they read the Wikipedia entry together.

'I see,' said Simon. 'I think. Could it be a copycat killer?'

'It's possible,' said Pippa. 'But there isn't any relation between people's names and the letters they're given. Janey Dixon got a letter A from a keyboard, Ritz Robertson got a badge with a B on it.'

'That makes it worse,' said Simon. 'C could be anyone. As could D. If they get that far.'

'You're right,' said Pippa. 'I'll phone Jim Horsley. We need to warn them.'

'Warn who?'

'The police, for one. But also the people who work at those offices. So far, they're the targets.'

***

'This is an unexpected pleasure,' said Jim Horsley. 'I assumed you were out on the town when you didn't reply to my texts.' A hum in the background suggested he wasn't at home.

'That's most unlikely and you know it.' Pippa paused.

'What do you think about the badge?'

A brief silence. 'I think we've got a wannabe serial killer on our hands.'

Pippa swallowed. Hearing someone else say what she was thinking made it even worse. 'Yes. And a copycat killer, maybe.' She explained about *The ABC Murders* and the copy missing from Much Gadding library.

'Well, now,' said Jim Horsley.

'Yes. Simon thinks the person might be trying to either send me a message or frame me.'

'That's rather worrying.' A pause, then the clink of a glass on a table. 'I'd like to pop down and discuss this with you, if you don't mind. I can be there in ten minutes.'

'Oh for heaven's sake, Jim, you're off duty!' said an exasperated voice in the background.

The noise from the phone quietened — Pippa assumed Jim was covering the mouthpiece — but she could still hear him. 'It's a murder case, Mandy, this is important.'

Mandy's response wasn't clear, but it didn't sound positive.

'Fine,' said Jim Horsley, and the phone unmuffled.

'I'm sorry to phone on a Saturday evening,' said Pippa. 'I'm sure you need time off —'

'Would you mind if I bring my partner?' he asked. 'She's a police officer too, so it wouldn't be breaking confidentiality.'

'Sure,' said Pippa. 'Why not.'

'See you soon.' And the call ended.

'He's coming, then,' said Simon.

'Yes. And he's bringing his partner. Who's also in the

police.'

'Some people have dinner parties on a Saturday evening,' said Simon. 'Some people get together to play board games. We shall serve them the remains of the lasagne and play Cluedo. Only with real people.' He got up too. 'I'll check we have spare wine and four glasses that aren't completely random. Just in case.'

'I'll polish the silver and get the napkin rings out,' said Pippa. 'I mean wipe the dining table and plump the cushions.'

'Got four glasses,' Simon called through from the kitchen. He returned with a cloth. 'Do you ever feel,' he said, as he lifted the placemats and wiped the table, 'that as we get older, life is growing more surreal?'

'All the time,' said Pippa, and went to remove toys and debris from the lounge carpet.

***

'I think that's them,' said Pippa, at a quiet tap on the front door.

Jim Horsley looked much the same out of uniform as he did in it, with a sea-green jumper instead of the regulation police one. 'Thank you for coming over,' said Pippa, then took in his companion as she stepped inside. 'I do hope we haven't interrupted anything special.' Mandy was the young woman who had sat next to Jim Horsley at the Much Gadding proms the year before; but the stripy top and jeans had been replaced by a floaty off-the-shoulder top, tight trousers, and spike-heeled boots. Her former brown bob, now shoulder-length and blonde at the ends, was done in the sort of casual beachy waves which

Pippa suspected had taken a good while to get right.

'Oh no, we were just down the pub,' said Jim.

'I can offer you a glass of wine,' said Pippa.

'That would be nice,' said Mandy.

'Not while I'm on police business,' said Jim. 'Maybe later. Oh yes, um, Pippa, this is Mandy. Mandy — Pippa Parker.'

'And I'm Simon, Pippa's husband.' Simon shook hands with them both. 'Shall we go into the lounge, or would you prefer the dining room?'

'Easier to work in the dining room, I think,' said Jim.

'I'll open the wine. Jim, would you like tea or coffee?'

'Um, tea would be nice. One sugar, please.'

'Told you,' said Pippa. 'We were talking about whether the police drink tea or coffee earlier,' she added, in response to Jim and Mandy's look.

'Tea for you, Pippa, or wine?' asked Simon.

Pippa sighed. 'Better stick to tea, I suppose. Have you eaten? There's lasagne if you want.'

'Oh no, we ate before the pub,' said Jim. 'Although I could probably fit in a small piece.'

'I'll warm it through, then,' said Simon. 'Mandy, lasagne for you?'

'Ooh no,' said Mandy. 'I'm off carbs. I probably shouldn't have the wine, but it is Saturday night.'

'Indeed it is,' said Simon. 'I'll be joining you.'

Mandy giggled. 'Good.'

'We'd better get on,' said Jim. 'Pippa, do you have a notebook I can borrow?'

'Of course.' Pippa led the way to the dining room and

handed her notepad to the policeman. 'You must feel lost without yours,' she said.

'Oh, I do. And naked without my hat.'

Mandy gave him a reproachful look, pulled a chair out for him and sat in the next one, moving it a little closer. Simon came through and handed her a glass of wine. 'Thank you,' she said, giving him a wide smile.

'No problem,' said Simon, retreating to the kitchen.

Pippa wrenched her attention back to the matter in hand. 'Tell me about Ritz Robertson's car.'

'Oh yes. The brake hoses had been loosened. The garage said there was no brake fluid at all.'

'Would that be easy to do?'

'Reasonably, with the right tool. It's a matter of loosening a nut with a spanner. But it isn't something you'd do in broad daylight.'

'I don't suppose it is.'

'Especially not with a car as conspicuous as Ritz's,' said Mandy.

'What sort of car does he drive?' asked Pippa.

'Haven't you seen the Ritzmobile?' Mandy laughed. 'It's a sky-blue convertible with *Ritz* on the bonnet in silver.'

'So everyone would know it was his. And if the top was down, it would be easy to slip the badge into the glove compartment. I see.' Pippa thought. 'Does he keep it in a garage at home?'

'He does,' said Jim Horsley. 'And he has a reserved space in the office car park, right outside the building. So if you were going to mess with his car early morning would probably be the best time, before the office staff are in.'

'So, do you think early Friday morning?'

'Seems reasonable,' said Jim. 'Ritz said he came in at six to prep for his show, and it would still have been dark then. The car park's tucked away behind the office, so no-one would be passing. And whoever did it loosened all the nuts just a bit. They wanted Ritz's brakes to work long enough to get him out of the car park, and fail when he really needed them.'

Pippa shivered.

'This'll warm you up,' said Simon, setting her mug on a coaster. 'But it does sound horrible.' He passed another mug to Jim.

'It is,' said Jim. 'We'll be checking the whereabouts of all the staff early on Friday morning. However that car park isn't locked, and there isn't CCTV. A member of the public could have sneaked in and done it.' He sighed. 'Now, what about this ABC murder thing?'

'Ooh, I loved that show,' said Mandy. 'So *dark*.'

'That was what I didn't like about it,' said Pippa.

Mandy's lip curled. 'I can't bear all those country houses and old ladies knitting, it's so false. Give me a proper gory story any day.'

'But it was nothing like the book,' said Pippa.

'Oh, the book.' Mandy drank some wine and set her glass down sharply on the coaster. 'Who has time for that?'

Pippa raised her eyebrows. 'The point is that the killer may be referencing the book. Or, I suppose, the series. There's been an *A* murder, and an attempted *B* murder, and we should be trying to prevent a *C* murder.'

'But we have no idea who C will be,' said Simon, putting a plateful of lasagne in front of Jim Horsley. 'It's pretty hot, watch out.'

'C will be someone who works in that building,' said Pippa. 'That's the only common thread we have.'

'Yes,' said Jim, blowing on a forkful of lasagne to cool it. 'And we need to do two things. First, close the building.'

'Really?' asked Simon.

PC Horsley nodded as he swallowed. 'Yes. The killer seems comfortable there, and moving everyone out might disrupt them.'

'It'll definitely be disruptive,' said Pippa. 'Gerald Tamblyn'll go mad.'

'He'll like my other idea, though,' said Jim Horsley. 'The inspector agrees. And he'll agree even more when he hears your ABC idea.'

'Go on then,' said Simon. 'Don't keep us in suspense.'

They watched the policeman dispose of another forkful of lasagne. 'Go public,' he said, eventually. 'Mount a campaign. Put everyone on the alert. That'll make it harder for the killer to operate, and hopefully we can close them down.'

'That makes sense,' said Pippa.

'Glad you approve,' Jim replied. 'There's another bit that you won't approve of.'

Pippa's eyes widened. 'Oh?'

'Mm-hm. The library thing tells me that the killer has cottoned on to you, and I take that seriously. I think you should come off this case.'

'*What?*'

'I know. Certainly you shouldn't be seen coming in and out of police stations, or, indeed, the newspaper building. We can keep you informed without face-to-face meetings.' Jim disposed of the last bite of lasagne and scraped his fork round the plate. 'And you probably shouldn't poke around asking questions, either.'

'Yeah,' said Mandy. 'When civilians get involved they usually end up causing trouble.'

'Thanks,' said Pippa.

'You'd still be involved,' said Jim, 'just not directly.'

'Does she have to be involved?' asked Mandy.

'Hundred percent success rate,' said Jim. 'I wouldn't bet against Pippa. And that was a delicious lasagne.'

'Must be lovely to have the time on your hands to cook food from scratch,' said Mandy, glaring.

'Simon made it, actually,' said Pippa. 'I was too busy floating between the nail bar and the hairdresser's.'

Jim grinned, then straightened his face hastily as Mandy transferred her glare to him. 'If you two have quite finished,' she said, draining her glass and getting up, 'let's get back to our night out. Thanks for the wine,' she said to Simon, smiling sweetly.

'Any time,' he replied. 'Lovely to meet you.'

'You too.' The smile broadened. 'And you, of course, Pippa. I've heard so much about you, and now we've met in the, um…' Her gaze settled on the waistband of Pippa's jeans. 'Flesh.'

'I'm sure the feeling's mutual,' said Pippa. 'I'll think over what you've said, Jim.'

'Please do.' Jim Horsley looked as if he wanted to put on his policeman's hat. 'Goodnight. And watch out for serial killers.'

'I always do,' said Simon. 'Thanks for coming down.'

Pippa waited till the door had closed behind them before pouring herself a glass of wine. 'I *need* this,' she murmured, taking a gulp.

'Maybe you do,' said Simon, kissing her. 'But you should listen to Jim Horsley. You're the only wife I've got, and I don't want you being murdered.'

'I'm not sure I trust his judgement,' muttered Pippa. 'Look at his taste in girlfriends.'

Simon stared at her.

'What?'

He snorted, then leaned in to kiss her again.

CHAPTER 13

'I still don't think you should go,' said Simon.

'The inspector wants me there to observe; he said so. And you'll enjoy doing the school and nursery run for a change.'

'I'm sure I shall, but that isn't the point.'

'I'll be fine. No one will even notice me. And if I'm worried I'll come straight home and hide with a baseball bat.'

Simon sighed. 'Just text to let me know you're safe, OK?'

'OK.' She kissed him, picked up her bag, and let herself out.

The road to Gadcester was busy with commuters again. Pippa parked the Mini in a different car park. Round the corner was a small, dingy cafe, *The Coffee Pot*. A bell jangled as she went in.

Inspector Fanshawe was sitting in the back corner, nursing a cappuccino. 'Morning,' said Pippa, sitting opposite.

'Good morning. Can I get you a drink?'

'No, I had one before I left.' Truthfully, Pippa hadn't been able to manage anything else.

The inspector surveyed the cafe, which was quiet. 'Are you still up for this?'

'I think so,' said Pippa. 'I mean, yes.'

'Good.' The inspector reached under the table and handed Pippa a carrier bag. 'The bathroom's through that bead curtain,' he said. 'Second on the left.'

'Thanks,' said Pippa. 'Do you come here often?'

'More than you'd think,' said the inspector. 'I'll brief you when you return.'

Inside the bag was a navy polo shirt with *MB Cleaning Services* embroidered on the pocket in green, a matching green tabard, and a green baseball cap with the company name in navy. *At least I'm coordinated*, thought Pippa, as she tucked her hair into the cap. The finishing touch was a pair of black-framed glasses with plain lenses.

'You'll do,' said the inspector as she sat down. 'I certainly wouldn't give you a second glance.'

'Thanks,' said Pippa.

'You know what I mean.' Inspector Fanshawe peered at her. 'You look . . . tired.'

'I'm not wearing any make-up,' said Pippa. 'That's probably it.'

The inspector's eyebrows knitted. 'I didn't think you did anyway.'

'Men don't understand these things,' said Pippa. 'Tell me what I need to know.'

The inspector sipped his coffee. 'You begin work at 8.30. Sign in at reception as Jane Harmer. If anyone asks, Jodie has a family emergency and you're covering her shift. With me so far?'

Pippa nodded.

'The cleaning trolley and the vacuum are in a cupboard by the lift. Start work in the boardroom. Inspector Gannet and I shall arrive there at nine thirty, and ask you to remain for an all-staff meeting. Stay in the background, and observe the reactions of the staff. I plan to keep the meeting fairly short, and then staff will head to their offices to pack up. I would like you to clean the main newspaper office, and if possible, the radio station offices too.'

'I presume not in the actual studio,' said Pippa.

The inspector gave her a withering look. 'No. But listen to as many conversations as you can while remaining unobtrusive. Your shift finishes at half past eleven. Sign out, and find somewhere to take your uniform off before returning to your car.'

'Got it,' said Pippa. 'I may not be able to report back straightaway, as I'll have to pick Ruby up.'

'Righto,' said the Inspector. 'Send me a message when you're safely home.'

'I'll add you to the list,' said Pippa. 'But I'd better get moving or Jane will be late.'

***

Diane looked up without interest as Pippa swung through the door. 'Jodie off again?'

'Family emergency,' muttered Pippa as she wrote *Jane Harmer* in rounded letters in the visitors' book.

110

Diane snorted and handed her a large key on a poodle keyring. 'Make sure you bring it back.'

There was only one cupboard near the lift. Pippa unlocked the door and found a loaded cleaning trolley and a round, squat vacuum. She wheeled them out, returned the key and then set about getting the trolley into the lift, which was the last place it wanted to go. It swerved, caught on the flooring, and threatened to tip over, until Pippa wondered if the killer had tampered with the trolley as well as Ritz's car. 'Your dad was probably a supermarket trolley,' she told it as she finally manoeuvred it into the lift and thumped the button for the second floor.

No one was in the boardroom. Pippa walked to the windows, which took up most of one side of the room, and gazed down at the street below. People were hurrying — it was too early for shoppers — and some of them were coming into the building. Pippa had checked out staff photos on the web. The tall woman with curly dark hair might be Jenny Mace, and the chubby fair-haired man in a blue polo shirt looked like Stewart Burgess, the mid-morning DJ.

She'd see them all soon enough, anyway. Pippa searched for a window-cleaning spray and got to work. After that she polished the table, dusted and straightened the framed awards and front pages on the walls, and wiped the cupboards, paying particular attention to the handles. *It's rather nice cleaning when there isn't mess or chaos*, she thought, listening to the vague sounds of people talking and phones ringing and doors closing downstairs.

But the murderer is down there. They must be…

Was it a man or a woman? A man seemed more likely, given the force that must have been used to kill Janey Dixon. And messing with car parts definitely seemed more masculine — though, Pippa thought, she shouldn't stereotype. *My job is to keep my eyes and ears open.*

Pippa checked her watch. *9.20.* She plugged the vacuum in and switched it on.

It was exceptionally loud; so much so that she jumped when the door opened and Inspector Fanshawe walked in, followed closely by PC Gannet.

'Could you stop that, please,' PC Gannet said loudly, giving no sign of recognition.

Pippa switched off the vacuum and unplugged it.

'Thank you,' said the inspector, winking. 'We're about to have a staff meeting but since you work in this building too, we'd like you to stay. You can carry on afterwards.'

'Yes, sir,' said Pippa, and winked back. PC Gannet ran a finger along the table and inspected it. Pippa wiped the table where he had touched it. PC Gannet frowned at her.

Feet sounded on the stairs, and the lift pinged outside.

Pippa tugged the peak of her cap down and braced herself. However, the people coming into the room were much too busy eyeing the policemen and muttering amongst themselves to pay any attention to the cleaner standing beside the trolley. The newspaper people stood together; the radio station people stood together; two separate communities united by one building.

'Is everyone here?' asked the inspector.

'Mr Tamblyn's on his way,' piped a young man in a white shirt, shiny grey trousers, and a plain tie, whom

Pippa guessed must be Sean Davies. 'He's finishing a call.'

'All right. And from the radio station?'

'Had a quick word with Tony and his producer Phil,' said Stewart Burgess. 'They'll be up just after 9.30. Tony's segueing into a fifteen-minute megamix after the news.'

'I see. In that case I shall be brief.'

Gerald Tamblyn strolled in. 'Sorry about that. You can start now.'

'We're waiting for one more,' said PC Gannet, and the editor huffed and fidgeted.

Pippa leaned against the cupboard, arms folded, trying not to look too interested in proceedings. Graham Dean leaned across to Jenny Mace. 'What d'you think they've come to say?' he muttered.

She shrugged, eyes on the policemen. 'Guess we'll find out soon.'

Two men burst through the door. The first wore a long-sleeved maroon T-shirt emblazoned with the name of a band Pippa had never heard of, and his dark hair was carefully arranged. The second man was tall and broad, almost like the other man's minder, and slightly breathless. 'We're good till nine forty-five,' said the first man. 'Can't risk dead air.'

'Dead air isn't the worst that could happen, Tony,' Inspector Fanshawe observed. Then he stepped forward. 'I'm sure you're hoping I've come to tell you we've arrested the person who killed Janey Dixon and tampered with Ritz Robertson's car.' He paused. 'Unfortunately, we haven't. But we think the two incidents are connected, and there is reason to believe more attempts will be made on

113

lives of people who work in this building.' A buzz of consternation rose from his audience. 'Therefore we are closing it.'

'Don't be ridiculous!' cried Gerald Tamblyn. 'What, someone's bumping people off to get control of the building?'

'This isn't Scooby Doo, Mr Tamblyn,' the inspector replied. 'But the killer seems very comfortable here. I don't think we should let a murderer get comfortable, do you?'

'Why wasn't I informed of this in advance?' the editor snapped.

'I thought it fairer to let all staff know at the same time.' The inspector appeared entirely unruffled. 'After all, it affects everyone.'

A small man in a navy suit stepped forward. 'I shall contact other radio stations in our group and see if anyone can accommodate us. It may mean splitting people between station premises, or possibly syndicating some of their content. I'm sure we can do something. There's always the OB vehicle if we're really stuck.'

'Thank you, Brendan.' The man nodded and stepped back. The staff around him looked either relieved or expressionless — possibly, Pippa thought, depending on how convenient the new arrangements would be for them.

'Most of us can work from home or out of our cars,' said Gerald Tamblyn, grudgingly. 'Good job we don't print the damn thing here. It'll make our job twice as hard, though.'

'What about me?' asked Sean.

'And me!' cried Diane.

'We'll work something out,' said the editor, in a tone that lacked conviction.

'Excellent,' said the inspector. 'I'll give you the rest of the day to make arrangements and pack, but from five o'clock today this building is closed, and will remain so until further notice. And before I let you go — be vigilant. Please. There's a murderer on the loose, and there's no pattern to what they're doing. Don't work late on your own. Take care on your way to and from work. Watch what you eat and drink, even. Because for all you know, the murderer could be in this room right now.'

Silence fell as people sneaked surreptitious glances at each other.

'Brendan, Gerald, if I could have a word with you both…'

'Of course,' said Gerald Tamblyn. 'Right everyone, back to work.'

Tony Jeffries and Phil hurried off, followed by the rest, in twos and threes, eyeing other groups as they dispersed. 'I'm not getting in that lift,' Diane muttered, as she strolled off.

Pippa took the brake off her trolley, picked up the vacuum, and after two goes, got the trolley through the door. 'In your own time,' said Gerald Tamblyn, tapping his foot.

'Sorry,' muttered Pippa, and gave him a V-sign once the door was safely closed.

People were already buzzing around in the main newsroom. Sean was carrying plastic boxes to each desk, and the reporters were pulling files from the cabinets. Pippa wheeled the trolley to the windows and took out her spray bottle.

'What about Janey's stuff?' Graham asked Darren Best, who was frowning at a desk calendar.

'No point,' said Darren. 'She kept it so much to herself that I hadn't a clue what she was working on till she filed it. And I bet it's passworded anyway.' He sighed. 'Maybe we can pick up arts content from another paper in the group.'

Jenny scowled. 'No, Darren. Don't give Gerald more excuses for "efficiencies".' She unplugged her docking station and put it in a box. 'I hope tech support can get us up and running.'

Pippa moved to the next window.

'I want to know what the police are doing,' said Sean, clunking down a stack of boxes. 'We could probably find the murderer before that lot.'

'I don't suggest you try, Sean,' said Graham. 'Unless you want to be bumped off, of course.'

'I'd like to see him try,' said Sean, flexing a bicep. 'I'm a lot fitter than Janey or Ritz. I wouldn't fancy his chances.'

'Don't be a hero, Sean,' said Jenny, wearily.

'Yeah, well,' muttered Sean, turning away. 'You've still got a job.'

'It's only temporary, Sean,' said Jenny. 'We'll be back in no time.'

'We'd better be,' said Sean. 'And I'll be doing some investigating of my own, when I'm not at the gym. I bet I can run rings round the real police.'

Pippa finished the second window and surveyed the room. There wasn't any point in vacuuming a floor covered with boxes, or wiping desks in the process of being cleared. *Off to the radio station*, she thought.

Their office was much smaller; presumably there weren't usually so many people in all at once. The back wall was glass, and through it Pippa glimpsed Stewart Burgess, headphones on, talking into a microphone, while behind another glass partition was Phil. She set to work on the windows again.

'It's just worrying,' Tony Jeffries was saying to a DJ Pippa didn't recognise, as he unhooked a silver disc from the wall. 'They'll take any excuse to merge stations, and then we'll be Gadcester and Mumford FM, or something. All prerecorded and a playlist of whatever the advertisers decide they want. Which'll probably be wall-to-wall Ed Sheeran and whatever else the *primary demographic* are into. I mean, we're already prerecorded from half ten till six am.'

'You're catastrophising, Tony,' the other man replied, mildly.

'I'm bloody not, Steve,' Tony retorted. 'You'll be back on the mobile disco before you know where you are.'

'I ruddy won't. And I bet you'll still be handing over to me at seven-thirty pm in six months' time.' Steve laughed. 'Why are you taking that disc down?'

'I earned that. Me. For all you know, we might never come back.' Tony wrapped the framed disc in bubble wrap and slotted it lovingly into a box.

The rest of the people there were packing quietly; but Pippa sensed they were listening to Tony. Again, there was little more she could do. She tried Gerald Tamblyn's office, and Brendan's, but was waved away irritably by Gerald and apologised to by Brendan. So Pippa vacuumed reception, wiped the counter, and packed up.

'Short day today,' said Diane, as she signed out. 'But what can you do, eh? Send Jodie my regards.' She sighed and returned to her magazine.

Pippa changed in a department-store toilet and drove home. She texted the inspector, and Simon, and as she had half an hour before pick-up time, made a cup of tea. *I must write it all down,* she thought. *What was said, the mood in each office...* She sighed, and examined her hands, which felt dry and a little raw. No doubt Mandy would be delighted to know she had spent a whole morning working. But Pippa wasn't sure what, if any, good it had done.

CHAPTER 14

'So what do you think?' asked Caitlin, as they moved the play kitchen into the middle of the church hall.

Pippa was glad that her expression was obscured from view by a plastic grill. 'About what?' she asked.

'Don't give me that,' said Caitlin. 'The murders! You know, the QWERTY Murders!'

'Is that what they're calling them?' Pippa eyed the door. It was five to ten, but the chances of early birds were high. There had been a lot of new faces at the last couple of meetings, and they tended to be on time, rather than sloping in as Lila and Sam had done. Their eagerness was disconcerting.

'It was all over the paper this morning,' said Caitlin. 'Even though Ritz was only an attempted murder.'

Gerald Tamblyn had taken the inspector at his word. That morning's *Chronicle* and social media updates had been largely devoted to spreading the word, with detailed breakdowns of when and where the crimes were thought to

119

have been committed, appeals to the public to come forward, and quotes from Inspector Fanshawe and PC Gannet (whose photo made him look sinister). The one thing which had not been shared was the new location of Gadcester FM and the newspaper staff.

'Ritz would probably be upset at his car crash being described as "only" anything,' said Pippa. 'Still, QWERTY Murders sounds good. Especially as *The ABC Murders* was already taken.'

The missing book still bothered her. She had examined shopping bags, random drawers, and even the veg rack, but the book remained obstinately unfound.

'And what's your view?' asked Caitlin, also glancing at the door.

'I don't have a view,' said Pippa. 'Nothing to do with me, no more trips to the police station.'

'Pull the other one,' said Caitlin.

'I'm being vigilant, the same as any other public-spirited Gadcestershire citizen,' said Pippa. 'And don't you poke about either. Whoever it is means business, and you don't want to be letter C.'

'Mmm,' said Caitlin. 'I'm probably safe, as my name actually begins with a C. You have to admit, it's a bit tenuous.'

'It is, rather,' said Pippa. 'But we can't underestimate whoever's doing this. So far they've got away with two crimes.' The door creaked open and she went to greet another new face.

Caitlin tried to engage Pippa again at break time, but Pippa pleaded kitchen duties, since the new people still

120

needed, as she put it, breaking in. 'They're ever so willing,' she said, out of the side of her mouth, 'but they don't know where anything is.'

'And to think, Pippa,' Caitlin replied, 'that two years ago you were a new girl.'

'Ah yes, in the days before murder came to Much Gadding.'

'Mmm.' Caitlin regarded her speculatively. 'Have you ever thought that you might be the problem?'

'Do shut up and watch Ruby,' said Pippa, heading for the kitchen. There it was easy to explain the urn and point to cupboards and find the sugar and the cake stand, and *not to think about the murders*.

Following her undercover mission, Pippa had managed to ring Inspector Fanshawe when Ruby went down for an afternoon nap. 'Hello, Mrs Parker,' he said, 'any feedback?' And Pippa had given him the gist of what she had seen.

'I see,' he had commented. 'So some worries about, what, redundancies and mergers?'

'I don't think it was anything more than you'd expect,' she said. 'They sound under pressure, but no-one did anything suspicious.'

He sighed. 'I didn't think they would. All right, Mrs Parker, thank you for your time —'

'Oh, there was one thing,' said Pippa, remembering the office junior carting boxes around for the reporters. 'Sean Davies said he might do a bit of investigating.'

'Oh no,' said Inspector Fanshawe wearily. 'If there's one thing I can't stand it's members of the public playing detective.' A pause. 'Present company excepted of course, Mrs Parker.'

'He's on the spot,' said Pippa.

'No he isn't,' said the inspector. 'Without an office there's no need for a junior, so he's on paid leave for now. If he has any sense he'll get on and enjoy it.'

'How did the bosses seem?' asked Pippa.

The inspector considered. 'Mr Tamblyn is enjoying the drama. Brendan Shirrell is a businesslike sort of chap and I imagine he will handle the matter in that way rather than taking it personally.'

'Could either of them be the murderer?' asked Pippa.

'Nope. Gerald Tamblyn was with friends at the time of Janey Dixon's death; that's confirmed. Brendan Shirrell was at a corporate event in the next county on Wednesday night, and with his wife at their lodge in Scotland from Thursday night to Saturday. The photos on their mobiles prove it, and we've spoken to the staff at the complex too.'

'I'm glad about Brendan Shirrell,' said Pippa. 'He seems nice.'

'So you'd prefer Mr Tamblyn to be the murderer?' There was the ghost of a smile in the inspector's voice.

'I didn't say that!' cried Pippa.

A wail from upstairs. 'Oh no, I've set Ruby off. Better go.'

'You had.' Inspector Fanshawe still sounded amused. 'If you have any bright ideas, do let us know.'

***

Sheila met Pippa at her front door looking unusually eager. 'Oh I *am* glad to see you, Pippa,' she said. 'And you

122

too, Ruby, of course.'

'Good,' said Ruby, wriggling out of Pippa's grasp and walking into Sheila's kitchen. 'Can I have a biscuit?'

'In a moment, dear. Do come in, Pippa.'

'I can't stay long,' said Pippa, 'I have to be at Higginbotham Hall by half past one.'

Sheila followed Ruby into the kitchen and lifted down the biscuit barrel. 'So long as you eat it nicely on a plate, dear, and don't make crumbs.' She handed Ruby a pink wafer on a plastic plate.

'Thank you,' said Ruby, with a hint of doubt in her voice, and went into the lounge.

'So what do you think about the *murders*?' Sheila mouthed the last word.

'There's only been one,' said Pippa. 'I don't know. And I really must dash.' She dropped a kiss on Ruby's forehead. 'I'll be back by three,' she called, and made a run for it before Sheila got her in a headlock or found the thumbscrews.

It's nice to be doing something unconnected with murder, she thought, as the Mini climbed the gravel drive to the Hall. However, Lady Higginbotham's worried face and twisting hands indicated far more distress than Caitlin or Sheila had shown about the possibility of a serial killer in their midst. She was also dressed in what appeared to be a new and possibly itchy cashmere jumper.

'Should I ask Beryl to do afternoon tea?' were her first words.

'It's just after lunch, Lady Higginbotham,' said Pippa. 'The poor wedding inspector probably gets plied with food at every visit.'

Lady Higginbotham surveyed the morning room. It was immaculate, with a beautiful new rug, fresh flowers, and no sign of damp. 'I never was sure about that shade of cream,' she said, eyeing the walls.

'The inspector's deciding whether your home is a suitable wedding venue,' said Pippa. 'They won't be critiquing your choice of wallpaper.'

'I suppose not.' Lady Higginbotham sighed. 'But first impressions are so important. I think I'd like some tea.' She crossed the room decisively and picked up the phone. 'Could you make tea, Beryl?'

'Out of curiosity, Lady Higginbotham, how many cups of tea have you had today?'

'Oh, umm…' The worried expression left Lady Higginbotham's face as she calculated. 'Oh dear. Sorry, Beryl, forget the tea. Unless you'd like a cup?' She raised her eyebrows.

'I'm fine,' said Pippa. 'I might have one when the inspector comes.'

'Sorry to bother you, Beryl.' Lady Higginbotham put the receiver down softly then picked at the cuff of her jumper. Pippa fought the urge to tap her wrist. 'Sorry, Pippa,' she said. 'I'm a bit edgy.'

'I'd never have guessed,' said Pippa, smiling.

Lady Higginbotham looked pleased for a moment, then rather crushed. 'It isn't every day that your home gets judged by a complete stranger,' she said.

The doorbell pealed and they waited for Beryl's footsteps. After two seconds Lady Higginbotham was twitching. 'Maybe I should go,' she said. 'The inspector might get cross if they have to wait too long. Or even go away. And then we'll have to start all over ag —'

'Beryl's coming now,' said Pippa.

Beryl clacked past — was she dressed up too? — and the front door opened without its customary creak. *They have been busy*, thought Pippa.

'Oh *hellooo*,' said Beryl, in her best telephone voice.

'Lady Higginbotham, I presume?' It was a female voice. London or maybe Essex, Pippa couldn't decide.

'Oh no, I'm the housekeeper,' said Beryl, and let out a little giggle. 'You must be the inspector. I'll take you to Lady Higginbotham, she's in the morning room.'

Beryl tapped at the door. Lady Higginbotham swallowed, audibly. 'Come!' she called, with a slight quiver in her voice, and stood up.

The door opened to reveal a small young woman with platinum-blonde hair in a quiff which added perhaps another two inches to her height. 'Good afternoon,' she said, smiling.

'Good afternoon,' said Lady Higginbotham warily. 'Welcome to Higginbotham Hall. I'm June Higginbotham.'

'I'm Daisy Franks, the venue inspector.' She advanced to shake hands. 'Don't take this the wrong way, Lady Higginbotham, but I half-expected you to be wearing a crinoline or a wedding dress. The Hall looks like that sort of place.'

'Oh dear me no!' said Lady Higginbotham, and let out a sound somewhere between a giggle and a hiccup.

'I'm Pippa Parker,' said Pippa, shaking hands. 'I help

out with events.'

The inspector turned to Lady Higginbotham. 'Could you show me the rooms you plan to use?'

'Of course. This is the morning room...' As Lady Higginbotham explained, Daisy Franks nodded at intervals, with an air of polite encouragement. *She must do this sort of thing all the time*, thought Pippa. But she kept her fingers crossed.

They went from the morning room into the hall, the dining room, the drawing room, and finally what Lady Higginbotham called the Long Room, a gallery-like room with French doors leading onto the lawn which Pippa had only seen once before. 'We couldn't use it yet, of course,' Lady Higginbotham said, waving a hand at the peeling wallpaper and threadbare curtains. 'But when we've decorated... And we could use it for receptions too.'

'You could,' said Daisy Franks. 'Although receptions aren't my job. Is that all the rooms?'

'I . . . think so.' Lady Higginbotham looked at Beryl, who nodded decisively.

'Right then.' Daisy Franks pulled a folder from her bag, took out a sheet, and began to tick. 'The good news is that in principle I'm perfectly happy to approve Higginbotham Hall as a venue for non-religious marriage ceremonies.'

Lady Higginbotham let out a huge sigh of relief and beamed.

'But,' said Daisy, 'there are a couple of things.'

Lady Higginbotham deflated still further.

'What sort of things?' asked Beryl, suspiciously.

'Nothing major.' A brief smile. 'I have your up-to-date

fire risk assessment, but what I don't have is a plan to address the issues. Things like signage for escape routes, a designated assembly point, and making sure that at least one of the doors leading outside is easy to open.'

'I'm sure we can fix that,' said Pippa.

'Good. The other thing is that I haven't seen any sign on your property that you are applying to become a wedding venue. Did you get the notice we sent?'

Lady Higginbotham looked blank. 'I don't remember seeing one.'

'Good job I brought a spare then.' Daisy Franks reached into the folder and handed over a laminated sheet. 'This needs to go up somewhere people can see it for twenty-one days. The application's on the web and we've had no objections, but we have to follow the law. Put the notice up, send me a nice action plan with bullet points and dates, and in twenty-one days I'll rubber-stamp your application.' She grinned. 'Leave it too long, and you'll end up waiting an extra month.'

'Is that how it works?' asked Lady Higginbotham, eyes wide.

'Not usually,' replied Daisy. 'But I'm backpacking round Europe for a month, and knowing our office, I'll come back to a pile of paper three feet high. So be warned.'

'Oh dear,' said Lady Higginbotham faintly, as they watched Daisy Franks march down the drive. 'More things to do.'

'We can do one of them now,' said Beryl, going to the morning-room desk and pulling out a packet of Blu-Tack.

'I'll stick the notice on the front door.'

'Pippaaaa,' said Lady Higginbotham, 'would you mind doing an action plan, if I send you the fire risk assessment?'

Pippa sighed. 'I'll have a go.' She pulled out her notebook and scribbled the points Daisy had mentioned. Underneath she added a note to herself: *Get Beryl to remind Lady H to send the assessment.* While Lady Higginbotham always meant to do her admin, that didn't mean it always happened. She glanced at her watch and stifled a rude word. 'I must go. School pick-up.'

'Always so busy.' Lady Higginbotham smiled.

'I'm afraid so,' said Pippa, getting up. 'Don't forget to send the assessment.'

'I won't!' Lady Higginbotham replied.

Beryl saw her out. 'I'll try and make her do it this afternoon,' said Beryl, under her breath. 'If I can divert her from wallpaper and carpet brochures.'

'Good luck,' said Pippa, and ran down the drive to the Mini.

CHAPTER 15

Pippa was still awaiting Lady Higginbotham's email on Wednesday morning. Presumably the lure of redecorating the Long Room had been too strong for Beryl to combat. She pulled out her phone and texted: *Please could you send me the fire risk assessment? I have some free time this morning and can work on it. Pippa x*

She sighed, and returned to flicking through the pages of door-pass codes. They still weren't communicating much, except... Had Janey been at work on the Tuesday, or not?

On impulse she rang the number for Much Gadding police station, but got the answering machine. Jim Horsley must be at Gadcester. She debated ringing his mobile . . . but no. That would look odd. Much better to text Inspector Fanshawe, since her last conversation had been with him.

The reply came swiftly. *Yes she was in work. Why?*

Her fingers flew over the keyboard. *There's no record of Janey's pass being used on Tuesday. The last record is*

Monday morning.

By return: *Interesting. I'll get Jim or Gabe to check the statements.*

Gabe? Presumably that was PC Gannet. Somehow it had never occurred to Pippa that he had a first name. He seemed to have been born a PC. Gabriel Gannet. She snorted. Then again, Pippa Parker wasn't much better.

Pippa's phone lit up, but this time it was Serendipity. *Are you free to talk?*

Pippa sighed, then texted back. *Sure, are you OK?*

Maybe. See you in 10 x

***

'She texted me,' said Serendipity, looking out at the garden where Monty was worrying fallen leaves.

'Your mother?'

'Yes. I'll show you.' Serendipity came round the table and Pippa read: *I'm sorry you don't want to do the show with us. It would have been a nice opportunity to get together as a family. Heal old wounds. Love you always, Mummy x*

'That's nice,' she said, then saw Serendipity's expression.

'She's up to something,' said Serendipity, with uncharacteristic viciousness.

'Are you sure?' asked Pippa.

'*Yes*,' said Serendipity, locking her phone so that the message disappeared. 'She's never said sorry to me before in her life. I'm not sure she's said it to anyone.'

'Oh.' Pippa eyed her friend's scowl. Serendipity looked like a truculent teenager, and she recalled Marge's

130

comment about being the grown-up. 'Have you replied?'

'Not yet,' said Serendipity, staring at her phone as if it might bite her and she was ready to retaliate. 'Let her stew.'

'Oh gosh, that's a point,' said Pippa. 'I haven't contacted Suze since the day we got your mother a police escort. I meant to, but — you know, murder and stuff.'

Serendipity gave her a sidelong glance, then burst into giggles. 'Only you could use that as an excuse, Pippa!'

Pippa shrugged, palms up. 'I'll text her now and explain. If that's OK with you?'

Serendipity shrugged back. 'She's your friend. Maybe it'll calm things down.'

Pippa typed: *Hi Suze, sorry I haven't been in touch for a few days. I don't know if you've seen in the news, but a local journalist was murdered and there was another incident too. Hope you're well. Pippa x*

She showed it to Serendipity. 'Will that do?'

'I'd be calmed down,' said Serendipity.

'Then off it goes,' said Pippa, and pressed *Send*. 'Now, seeing as you're here and no-one else wants to talk to me, shall we go over the bookings for next month?'

They spent a pleasant half hour talking things through and compiling a to-do list, though Pippa found herself glancing at her phone every so often. No new message appeared, however.

'She's probably in a meeting,' said Serendipity. 'She seemed like that sort of person.'

'Or sulking,' said Pippa, getting up to make more coffee.

The phone buzzed while she was rinsing the mugs. 'I knew it!' she exclaimed, hurrying in and grabbing the phone. 'A watched phone never gets messages.'

Insp F: *Checked statements of newspaper staff. JD defo in office all day Tues, snappy and uncommunicative. Although not sure that was unusual.*

Pippa thought for a moment, then typed: *Did anyone say she'd gone in or out of the building with them?*

A pause, then: *No one mentioned it.*

Hmmm. Pippa rubbed the frown from between her eyebrows.

'I'll go and make that coffee,' said Serendipity.

'Thanks. Sorry.' She stared at the words on the screen. *Did Diane on reception say anything?,* she texted.

Didn't look at that one. Will check.

Pippa put the phone down and pushed her fringe out of her eyes. 'I swear this case gets worse, not better,' she said.

Another flash. **Insp F:** *And thank you. Your input is genuinely helpful, unlike some of the theories we've listened to over the last day or two.*

Pippa grinned. *Would that be Sean Davies?,* she replied.

The reply was almost instant. *How did you guess? In the end Gabe told him to stop phoning us or he'd come round and caution him for wasting police time.*

Serendipity came through with the coffee. 'What did Suze say?' she asked, putting a steaming mug in front of Pippa. 'Are you friends again?'

'It's Inspector Fanshawe,' said Pippa. She texted a final message — *I'll leave you to it then* — and as she was about to put the phone down, another message flashed up.

Insp F: *Oh, and Jim said to say hi.*

Pippa put the phone firmly out of reach. 'I'd turn it off, but what with school and nursery… Right, back to this list. Do we need biscuits?'

'I usually bake for the workshops,' said Serendipity, looking perplexed. 'Has anyone said there weren't enough?'

'I meant right now,' said Pippa. 'In fact, I'm making a business decision that we do.' She got up and went into the kitchen. The packet of chocolate Hobnobs which Jim Horsley had opened were in the biscuit barrel, along with Jammie Dodgers for the children as a marginally less messy option. Suddenly Pippa could smell Jim's blue jumper and the aftershave he used, feel the rough wool against her cheek and his arms around her. She closed her eyes for a second but that made it worse —

'Pippa… Pippa, your phone's ringing.'

Oh no. I can't face a conversation with Suze. 'Who is it?' asked Pippa.

'It says Insp F,' Serendipity called back.

'Oh good,' said Pippa, hurrying through with the biscuits. 'Maybe they've worked something out.' She put the biscuit barrel down and Serendipity handed her the phone. 'Hello?'

'It's ever so exciting,' Serendipity whispered. 'Like being in a TV drama.'

Pippa winced as a siren blared out. 'Sorry,' said

Inspector Fanshawe. 'Got the blues and twos on. Are you sitting down?'

Pippa sank into the nearest chair, her stomach in a knot. 'I am now,' she said.

'A dog-walker called in something suspicious in Gadcester Canal earlier. He said it looked like a body. The station sent an officer out assuming it was probably a bag of rubbish that someone had dumped, but the dog-walker was right. A body, on the bottom of the canal. They're pulling it out now and we're heading over.'

'Oh my God.' Pippa whispered. 'Where on the canal?'

'On the towpath leading out of Gadcester, towards Oxford. It's a quiet stretch, not overlooked, pleasant countryside. Popular with bikers and joggers.' Inspector Fanshawe sighed. 'I have a horrible feeling this is going to be C. Better go.' A pause. 'Oh, and don't even think about coming out here, Pippa.'

'Absolutely not,' said Jim Horsley's voice in the background.

'I won't,' said Pippa. 'Fingers crossed.' And the call ended. Her mouth was dry, and she automatically reached for her mug.

Serendipity was regarding her with huge, tragic eyes which reminded Pippa of Monty. 'They've found a body in the canal,' said Pippa. Her voice sounded flat to herself. 'Police are on their way.'

'Do you want me to stay?' asked Serendipity. 'Would it help?'

'I don't think anything will help,' said Pippa, half to herself. 'I doubt I'm up to conversation.'

'It puts my woes into perspective, doesn't it,' said Serendipity.

She appeared to be waiting for a response, but Pippa couldn't think of anything that wouldn't sound curt or rude. 'I'll go and get Monty,' Serendipity said. 'I'm so sorry, Pippa.'

Pippa sat alone, her coffee cold and the biscuit barrel unopened. There was nothing she could do to help. Another person had died, and she could make no sense of any of it. No-one could, at the moment. She searched up the plot of *The ABC Murders* again on her phone, but the words danced before her eyes, and she put the phone down. She wanted to cry, but there was no point in that either.

The phone rang. Pippa pressed *Answer* and put it to her ear without checking who it was.

'We're waiting for formal identification,' said Jim Horsley, 'but it looks like Sean Davies.'

'Oh no,' said Pippa. 'Do they know how it happened?'

'Whacked on the back of the head,' said the policeman. 'Skull's fractured. Dr Watson thinks it happened just a few hours ago. The body was still at the bottom of the canal, and — I won't say more than that. He was dressed in a tracksuit, and had headphones in.'

'So he could have been going for a morning jog.'

'Yes.' A pause. 'The inspector's on the way to his house. He lives — lived with his parents.'

Pippa blinked. 'I'm so sorry.'

'So am I,' said Jim. 'Anyway, if you think of anything, Pippa…'

'Of course,' said Pippa. 'Goodbye, Jim.'

She caught a couple of syllables as she pressed *End Call*. It had sounded something like 'and I,' but she couldn't be sure. It didn't matter now, anyway. Another person had died, and all the police in Gadcestershire, and all the public input, had been powerless to stop it.

Pippa jumped as her alarm shrilled. *Pick up Ruby alert*, it said. How long had she been sitting there? Another alarm would ring in fifteen minutes, but perhaps Ruby's chatter, and a nice lunch, and an afternoon of play would take her mind off what was happening by Gadcester Canal. She picked up her keys and reached for her phone to switch the second alarm off.

The phone buzzed and the screen lit up. A text.

Piglet: *Personal effects removed and bagged for examination by forensics. Key ring with 2 keys. Phone with headphones attached. Plastic tube of soluble vitamin C tablets, empty.*

Pippa blinked.

Another text. *I'm sure I don't need to tell you what that means.*

No, Pippa replied.

No one would take an empty tube of vitamin C tablets on a run.

The QWERTY Murderer had struck again.

CHAPTER 16

'Say bye bye to Alicia, Ruby.'

'Don't wanna go.' said Ruby, clinging to Alicia's tabard.

Traitor, thought Pippa. 'I'm sorry, honey, but you're not booked in.'

'Ohhhhhh,' whined Ruby as Pippa led her down the path. 'Why can't I stay?'

'Reasons,' said Pippa. 'Now, what would you say to a trip to Gadcester?'

'Not the museum!' cried Ruby.

'OK, not the museum,' said Pippa. 'But we *could* go to the bookshop and maybe get you a book?'

'Yay! Books!' Ruby skipped happily, her sticky little hand in Pippa's.

It'll be fine, Pippa told herself as she changed Ruby, found her a fresh top, and brushed her hair, which had got quite wild during her artistic endeavours. *Gadcester Canal is nowhere near the bookshop. And if the bookshop is on the same street as the police station, that isn't my fault.*

The drive into town was accompanied by the lunchtime show on Gadcester FM, which mainly consisted of a mild-sounding DJ trying to calm the irascible listeners who rang to complain about dog-fouling, council policy and the youth of today. She was relieved on his behalf when he put a record on, possibly so that he could have three minutes of peace and quiet. 'You're listening to *Lunch with Dave Adams* on Gadcester FM, and that was Take That with "Back for Good". I'm delighted to tell you that Ritz Robertson will be returning to breakfast from tomorrow! Welcome back, Ritz, we've missed you.' A chuckle. 'Tony Jeffries will be over the moon that he doesn't have to get up in the mornings any more! Enjoy your lie-in tomorrow, Tony! And this one's for you; "Wake Up Little Susie".'

Pippa snorted and changed the station.

She parked in a different car park from the one she had used on her last visit. It turned out to be twice the price, and she scrabbled in her purse for change. An hour would have to do. 'Come along, Ruby,' she said, quickening her step and feeling the little arm pulling her back. 'We have to be quick.'

'Wanna look at things,' said Ruby.

'Yes, but we can't stay long.'

'You put money in the thing!' Ruby stared up at Pippa accusingly.

'I know, but it's a hungry one.'

'Silly Mummy. It's not an animal.'

'That's me told,' said Pippa. 'Let's just go to the bookshop, shall we?'

They walked past the tables at the front piled with the

latest offers, and Pippa craned her neck to see the categories on the shelves beyond. 'Children's! Children's!' cried Ruby.'

'In a moment,' said Pippa. 'Let me find something first.'

She wandered through the shop until she found the crime section, and scanned the shelves for C. There were a good two rows of Agatha Christie, but no copy of *The ABC Murders*. 'I'll go and ask at the desk.'

The assistant stared at the area of shelving Pippa had indicated, then looked the title up on her computer. 'No, we're out of stock on that title,' she said. 'It must be popular at the moment. That would be the TV adaptation.'

Pippa resisted the urge to ask the assistant if she'd read the papers lately. 'Thanks,' she said.

'I could order it in for you?' the assistant said, with a hopeful expression. 'We could give you a ring when it's in…' But Ruby was already tugging Pippa towards the back of the shop, where beanbags and brightly-coloured carpet tiles signalled the children's section.

'Read a book, Mummy!' she cried, pulling one off the display rack, giving it to Pippa, and plumping herself down on a beanbag.

'Yes miss,' said Pippa, looking around for a chair, seeing none, and lowering herself carefully onto another beanbag.

One story became two, and then three, as Ruby plundered the shelves for more books. 'I'm stopping after this one,' said Pippa, 'and then you can choose one.'

'Want them all!' said Ruby, folding her arms.

'Hello,' said an amused voice some way above Pippa's head. She squidged herself round on the beanbag, and, craning her neck, saw Gerald Tamblyn, holding what Pippa mentally classified as 'a book club book'.

'Hello,' she ventured, and slid backwards as the beanbag sagged beneath her.

'Shall I read one?' he asked. 'You don't appear very comfortable.' He held out his hand for the book and, to his credit, did all the voices including the dragon and the nasty old witch.

Ruby listened spellbound, and clapped at the end. 'You're funny! Do another!'

'I'd love to,' he said, 'but I have to get back to work. Another day, another crisis.' He sighed.

Pippa couldn't tell if he knew about Sean Davies or not, so made a sympathetic noise. 'How are things?' she asked.

'Not good. Darren's handed in his resignation. Said he didn't want to be next.'

'I can understand that,' said Pippa.

'Funny really,' said the editor, scratching the side of his nose. 'The newspaper group wants efficiencies, but now I'm fighting to keep enough staff to run the paper. At this rate it'll be just me banging away at a laptop. Anyway —' He sighed again. 'I'll let you return to your dragons.'

Pippa checked her watch. 'At this rate the parking attendant will turn into a dragon. Come on Ruby, choose a book.'

'This one!' Ruby pointed at the story Mr Tamblyn had read. 'Do it properly, Mummy. Like him. With voices.'

'See what you've done,' said Pippa, and attempted to

hoist herself off the beanbag in a dignified manner. Mr Tamblyn, looking a little pained, extended a long thin hand, which Pippa took, and levered her upwards surprisingly easily.

'Um, thanks,' said Pippa, dusting herself off.

'My pleasure,' he said, smirking, and Pippa felt rather gratified that she didn't have to feel sorry for him any more and could return to her previous combination of dislike and suspicion.

***

The school playground was packed as usual at going-home time. Pippa led Ruby, still clutching her new book, towards the groups of parents gathered in front of Miss Darcy's door. 'Oh, hi Pippa,' said Imogen, waving to her. 'How was yours?'

'My what?'

'Parents' evening. Or did Simon go?'

'Parents' evening?!'

'You didn't go?' Imogen's eyes widened.

'I didn't know!'

Imogen opened her mouth to reply but the school bell shrilled and everyone faced their respective classroom doors. Pippa took a step back as the reception door opened, but Mrs Ridout the teaching assistant had already seen her. 'Oh Mrs Parker, Miss Darcy would like a word.'

'I'd love to, but —' Pippa indicated Ruby.

'Don't worry, I can keep a little one amused.'

She held her hand out to Ruby, who galloped over. 'Would you read me a story, please?' she asked, holding up her book.

'Of course, sweetheart, as soon as the children have gone.' Mrs Ridout gave Pippa an *isn't she adorable* look, and Pippa suppressed the urge to growl at her daughter's display of beautiful manners and correct sentence structure. *Now is not the time for that sort of thing, Ruby.*

Miss Darcy was sitting at her desk, waiting for Pippa's approach. 'I wanted to talk to you about parents' evening, Mrs Parker.'

'I'm sorry, I didn't know there was one.'

'We put a letter in all the children's school bags,' Miss Darcy said.

'Oh, I see. I don't think Freddie gave it to me.'

Miss Darcy's mouth squished up slightly. 'He probably forgot. We recommend that parents check school bags at least every other day. Otherwise it's so easy for things to be missed. Parents' evenings, permission slips...' She waved a hand. 'That sort of thing.'

'I'll try to remember in future,' said Pippa, feeling as if Miss Darcy might point to the corner and tell her to stand in it. Most of the children had dispersed, but Freddie was standing next to the teaching assistant, watching her. She waved, but he didn't wave back. In fact he looked embarrassed.

'Would you like feedback?' asked Miss Darcy. 'I don't have Freddie's books to hand, of course, that was yesterday, but —'

'Yes please,' said Pippa.

Mrs Ridout came over with Freddie and Ruby. 'Shall I take the children to the library, Miss Darcy?'

'Please.' Pippa watched them go, feeling as if she might

never see them again.

'Now, Freddie…' Miss Darcy tapped a pencil on her desk. 'He's doing very well,' she said then, with a smile. 'He can read some three-letter words, and he is beginning to write letters legibly. Sometimes they are backwards, but that's normal. His maths is up to standard, and he enjoys arts and crafts. He throws himself into PE and joins in with games. However…' She glanced at Pippa. 'He does seem to watch rather a lot of television.'

'Oh,' said Pippa. *She's rumbled MegaMoose.* 'Did Freddie mention that we went to a farm park at the weekend?'

'No, he didn't,' said Miss Darcy, thoughtfully. 'He did say that he'd watched the whole *SuperMouse* DVD, though.'

'Oh, is he back on *SuperMouse*?' cried Pippa. 'I kind of missed it.'

Miss Darcy looked horrified. Then she crossed to the line of pegs, found Freddie's, and pulled a small blue book from his school bag.

Oh no, thought Pippa. *Not the reading record.*

Miss Darcy flipped through it, then held it out to Pippa. 'Freddie made a good start, but in the last two weeks there have only been three entries. We do recommend that you read with your child at least three times a week.'

'I thought you said his reading was OK,' said Pippa.

'But we don't want him to fall behind, do we?' Miss Darcy closed the book and tapped it. 'Several parents read with their child *every night*.'

'I don't always remember to fill the book in,' said

Pippa, clutching at straws. 'And I've been busy at work.'

'Mm,' said Miss Darcy. She looked at Pippa, and Pippa looked back.

'Is there anything else?' asked Pippa. *Can I go now please, Miss?* had been the phrase that sprang to mind.

'If you check the school bag tonight you'll find a letter about a trip to Gadcester Aquarium,' said Miss Darcy.

Pippa took that as a no. 'Thank you for your time, Miss Darcy,' she said. 'Could you tell me how to find the library, please, so that I can collect the children.'

Miss Darcy got up. 'I'll take you,' she said. 'Parents can't really wander round the school unaccompanied.' She fetched Freddie's bag and coat, and handed them to Pippa.

Feeling thoroughly rebuked, Pippa followed her to the library where Freddie and Ruby sat enthralled as Mrs Ridout stalked up and down, quite obviously being a fire-breathing dragon. She didn't stop when she saw Pippa, but carried on till the last page was turned.

'Thank you, Mrs Ridout,' said Miss Darcy, as if such things were perfectly normal. 'Could you show Mrs Parker the way out, please?'

Freddie seemed rather sulky at first, but gradually his little hand relaxed in Pippa's as they walked down the corridor. 'Did Miss Darcy tell you off, Mummy?'

'Yes,' said Pippa. 'I've been naughty for not checking your school bag and not filling in your reading journal every night.'

Mrs Ridout snorted, then composed herself as the children looked over. 'Bless me,' she said.

'Indeed,' said Pippa. 'Thank you for entertaining the

children, Mrs Ridout.'

'It was a pleasure,' said Mrs Ridout. 'They sat and listened ever so nicely, even this little one.' She lowered her voice. 'I wouldn't worry too much.' They reached the reception area, and she pressed the exit button. 'Straight on from here.'

'Thank you,' said Pippa, and meant it.

'Tearoom?' asked Freddie.

'I'm tempted,' said Pippa. 'However, instead I'll take you straight home, check your school bag, and spend a few minutes reading with you. I don't want Miss Darcy coming after me.'

Freddie sighed, and stomped beside her in silence.

At home Pippa flicked on the kettle, got milk and biscuits for the children, and pulled her phone from her bag. At least it hadn't gone off while she was in with Miss Darcy. That would probably have led to one hundred lines.

Just one message, from Inspector Fanshawe:

No info in Diane's statement so rang her. She said Janey was waiting for her to open up on Tuesday. Janey said she couldn't find her pass, and it had been missing since the day before. She'd had to ring security to get out on Monday evening.

Pippa made tea, and took everything through to the lounge. Freddie read a couple of pages of his book, with help, and she praised him at the end. But when it came to writing in the reading record, she couldn't remember anything about the book or Freddie's reading at all. Her mind was on Janey Dixon's pass, and who might have taken it.

CHAPTER 17

Simon put his head round the dining-room door. 'It's Friday night, Pippa. Please put those papers away.' He held out a glass of red wine. 'The wine is caaaaalling you.'

Pippa sighed. 'This is the first chance I've had to look at any of it today. Ruby didn't even nap this afternoon, and I took the kids to the park after school like a good girl, I mean responsible parent concerned for her children's welfare.'

Simon came into the room, moved Pippa's papers out of reach, and put the wine in their place. 'That probably isn't such a bad thing. Let the police handle it. Look what happened to Sean Davies.'

'And will continue to happen if the QWERTY Murderer isn't stopped.' Pippa took a gulp from the glass and put it down. 'It isn't as if doing other things is helping. Everyone's talking about it. Jen had to call choir to order several times on Wednesday night, and playgroup yesterday was horrendous. And everyone wants to know what I think.'

Simon put his hand on hers. 'What do you think?'

'I don't know.' Pippa pushed her hair back and drank some more wine. 'Did I tell you I rang Ritz Robertson?'

'Steady on, there,' said Simon. 'What happened?'

'He isn't answering his mobile, so I managed to find his home number. His wife answered, sounding suspicious, and when she heard my name she cut me short. Ritz doesn't want to talk about what happened at all. She said he's really upset, understandably, that someone tried to kill him. He has no idea who would want to do such a thing, and neither does she.' Pippa sighed. 'I decided that doorstepping him with a bunch of flowers would be counterproductive.'

'Just slightly.' Simon eyed the papers. 'Do you think you're getting anywhere with it?'

'Nope. Apart from Janey Dixon, the staff followed a routine that week. The ones who come in early did so all week, the ones who stayed late did it consistently. And that in itself is a bit weird. As if everyone was determined to behave normally.' She shrugged. 'Or maybe I'm over-thinking it because I'm trying to find something out of place.' She sighed. 'It's so frustrating. All I get are little bits of information through texts or phone calls. There's nothing to grab hold of.'

'Ah, so that's why you need the wine,' said Simon. 'Come on, let's go and watch rubbish TV. No crime dramas, though.'

The doorbell rang, and he rolled his eyes. 'At this time?' He padded into the hall. Pippa took another fortifying sip

147

from the glass.

Simon returned with a smallish rectangular parcel and a puzzled expression. 'It's for you,' he said, handing it over.

'Oh yes.' Pippa put the package on the table.

'Aren't you going to open it?'

'I know what it is,' said Pippa.

'And what is it? I can see it's book-shaped.'

Pippa sighed. 'All *right*.' She tore the cardboard strip down the middle, opened the packaging and took out a paperback book. 'Mystery solved.'

Simon snorted. '*The ABC Murders*. I should have known.' He held out a hand. 'Come on. TV. You can start it tomorrow, if you absolutely have to.'

***

Pippa's phone rang as they were watching a comedy panel show. 'If that's the police, ignore it,' said Simon, without taking his eyes off the screen. 'I reckon I've got the answer.'

'It's Suze,' said Pippa. She wasn't sure whether she felt relief, apprehension, or a mixture of both. She sighed, pressed *Accept* and walked into the kitchen. 'Hello?'

'Hello, Pippa,' said Suze, sounding just as she usually did. 'How are you?'

'Um, all right. I suppose,' said Pippa. 'And you?'

'I thought I should probably ring you and apologise,' said Suze. 'I've been meaning to for a couple of days, but, you know, work.'

'Mm,' said Pippa.

'So I'm sorry that I said the things I did. About war. Because we're friends, when you blocked me I took it personally. It wasn't, of course, and I should have realised that. So I apologise for reacting as I did. I ought to have been more professional.'

'That's OK,' said Pippa. 'And if I did over-react, I'm sorry too.'

Suze laughed. 'I think we both did. But we shouldn't let business get in the way of our friendship.'

Pippa felt tension lifting from her. 'No, you're absolutely right.'

They were both quiet for a moment, and Pippa noted the unusual absence of background noise. 'Aren't you in a bar or a club or a restaurant or something?'

Another little laugh. 'I shall be in about half an hour. Just finishing up at work, and then I'll be done for the weekend. What are you doing?'

'The usual Friday night. Drinking wine and watching TV on the sofa.'

'Ah, a quiet night in.' Suze's tone suggested she had heard of the concept, but not experienced it. 'How are you getting on with your murders?'

'They aren't my murders. And there's been another one.'

'Oh dear. But you do seem to take them personally. And there *are* rather a lot of murders in the Much Gadding area since you went to live there.' Suze sounded amused.

'Maybe there always were and it's only now I'm here that people are noticing.'

'Mm. Anyway, I hope you solve all the murders, and I'll let you get back to your sofa. Bye, Pippa, bye, bye.' The call ended.

'What did Suze have to say?' asked Simon. 'Is she sending in the cavalry?'

'I think she's withdrawing troops,' said Pippa, settling into her place on the sofa and pulling Simon's arm round her.

'Oh. That's good.'

'Yes. I'll text Serendipity and let her know.'

'Oh yes, Serendipity.' Pippa's thumbs danced over the keyboard. 'Has her mum stopped stalking her?'

'Uh-huh. She even apologised by text. So we're good.'

'That must be a relief.'

'Yes, it is,' replied Pippa, still texting. She pressed *Send* and put the phone on the coffee table. 'Maybe one day I'll get back to doing my actual job.' She picked the phone up again and checked her email. 'Lady H still hasn't sent me that fire plan thing. Remind me to text her on Monday. Or maybe ring. In fact, I'll remind myself.' She opened the calendar on her phone, and set a reminder for 9.30 on Monday. 'There. Now let's return to our night off.'

'What a good idea,' said Simon. 'Of course, we could stop watching this and go upstairs.'

'Oh yes,' said Pippa. 'Then I could start my book.' She giggled at Simon's injured expression. 'Just kidding,' she said, and kissed him.

***

Pippa managed to get seventy-eight pages into *The ABC Murders* the next morning before Simon woke up, grumbled at her for having her bedside lamp on, rolled over, and went back to sleep.

So far, it wasn't helping. She sighed, switched the lamp

off and went downstairs to make a cup of tea.

The *Chronicle* newsfeed was full of Sean Davies's murder. His mother had said that he usually went for a jog at six thirty, returning about an hour later, and often ran by the canal. The section of the towpath where Sean had been murdered was a mile and a half from his house. Members of the public were urged to contact Gadcester CID if they had seen anyone on the towpath between six-thirty and eight o'clock, particularly if they had been carrying anything that might have been used as a weapon. Sightings of the murdered man were also welcomed, in order to pinpoint the time of death more exactly.

Pippa shivered, and made the tea. Then she went into the dining room and found her notebook.

QWERTY Murders, she wrote.

A — Janey Dixon. Works at Chronicle. Stabbed from behind with a spike, in the office, at around 6.45-7 pm.

B — Ritz Robertson. Works at Gadcester FM. Car tampered with, almost certainly in office car park, early in the morning. Result: car crash (luckily minor).

C — Sean Davies. Works at Chronicle. Hit on back of head and fell/pushed into Gadcester Canal while out jogging, some time between 6.45-7.30am.

D —

Logically D would be a radio station employee. Until Sean's murder, all the incidents had taken place at the office building that housed the newspaper and the station, but now —

Inspector Fanshawe had thought closing the building might stop the murderer.

Instead, they had widened their field of operations, and in doing so, become less predictable.

Pippa drew a line under D. *What links these people, apart from the building they work in?,* she wrote.

Janey Dixon — senior member of staff, workaholic, loner

Ritz Robertson — main presenter, flamboyant, a character, happily married

Sean Davies — office junior, lived at home with family, young, fit, confident, said he was going to investigate —

Pippa stared at the page. The first two victims were senior, long-serving members of staff. Sean was unmistakably the odd one out. Had he always been part of the QWERTY Murderer's plan, or had he been killed because he was on to something? Had his determination to investigate made the murderer nervous, and sealed Sean's fate?

'Pippa?' Simon called quietly from upstairs.

'I'm making a brew,' Pippa called back. 'Do you want one?'

'Ooh yes.'

Pippa put her notepad securely away, and went into the kitchen.

'How's the book?' Simon asked, when she came in with the mugs.

Pippa got into bed and settled herself before replying. 'It's great, but I'm not sure it's relevant.'

Simon raised an eyebrow. 'Really? After all that? I thought you said —'

'Maybe the ABC thing is a coincidence.'

'But it can't be.' Simon put his mug down. 'Otherwise why would the murderer have bothered to pinch the library copy and pin it on you?'

Pippa's cup wobbled. 'Oh my.' She stared at her husband. 'You're absolutely right.' She put her own mug down and picked up the book. 'And in that case I need to finish it to work out how.'

Simon heaved a deep sigh. 'How did I know that would be the answer?' he said, and nudged her.

'Ssh. Reading,' said Pippa.

CHAPTER 18

Pippa finally closed *The ABC Murders* at 9.52pm on Sunday. 'At last,' said Simon. 'Maybe I can get some sense out of you now.'

'I doubt it,' said Pippa. 'I still don't understand.'

'Lots of hard words?' asked Simon, and grinned.

'Very funny,' said Pippa. 'Although reading a chapter here and there all weekend probably wasn't the best way to experience it. I mean I still don't see why it's relevant, except for the ABC thing.'

'Maybe the murderer wants you to think it is,' said Simon, stretching. 'Anyway, I'm heading for bed. I've got an early start tomorrow. Breakfast meeting the other side of Gadcester.' He looked at Pippa. 'What's up?'

Pippa snorted and dropped the book onto the coffee table. 'You're absolutely right. I can't believe I didn't see it.'

'See what?' Simon offered her a hand and pulled her up from the sofa.

'It's a gigantic red herring. The murderer deliberately did the ABC thing and pointed me towards the book so I'd go off on the wrong track. There isn't any similarity between the book and what's going on in Gadcester at all!'

'Ah.' Simon picked the book up and read the back. 'So do you know what the right track is?'

'Um, no,' said Pippa, climbing the stairs. 'Not yet. But at least I know I was on the wrong one.'

She gasped, and Simon bumped into her. 'What now?' he asked.

'The murderer knows I read Agatha Christie books. They did this especially for me, to put me off. And I remember... When Janey Dixon did a profile of me, she put that in. The murderer's probably been looking me up in the newspaper archives, or found the piece on the web.'

'That isn't disturbing in the slightest,' said Simon. 'What are you doing now?'

'Texting Jim Horsley to find out if anyone has done a newspaper archive search on the web with me as a search term.'

'Would he be able to find that out?'

'No idea. But it's worth a try.'

* * *

Pippa woke to bright sunshine and the sound of buzzing the next morning. *Is there a bee in here?* was her first thought. However, the buzz was coming from her bedside table. She rolled over and stretched out her hand.

Google Alert: Serendipity Jones.

Pippa had set up an alert on Serendipity's name about a year ago, in order to keep track of any mentions in the press. Usually it only returned results from Serendipity's own blog, guest posts she had made on other people's blogs, or press releases Pippa had circulated. 'But I haven't sent anything out,' murmured Pippa, and opened the email. Then she wished she hadn't.

I'M DEAD TO MY DAUGHTER: How craft blogger Serendipity Jones cut off her family.

MY DAUGHTER WON'T EVEN SPEAK TO ME: New reality TV star Julia Skeffington-Jones reveals how the rift between crafting queen Serendipity Jones and her family began.

WE MISS YOU EVERY DAY, SERENDIPITY: Serendipity Jones's sister Araminta speaks out.

Pippa let out an inarticulate noise and dropped the phone onto the bed as Simon came in.

'That thing's been buzzing since six am,' he said. 'I don't know how you can sleep through it.'

'Never mind the QWERTY Murderer,' Pippa spat. 'If Suze were here right now I'd murder her with pleasure. The *snake!*'

'What's she done?' Simon sat on the bed and Pippa handed him her phone. 'Oh. I see.'

Pippa clutched her hair. 'I don't know whether to ring Serendipity and warn her, or wait in case she isn't awake yet. I don't know what she'll do when she sees this. Run away, probably.'

'In that case, get in touch,' said Simon. 'The last thing you want is for her to do something silly.'

Pippa's fists clenched and she grimaced as the pull on her hair increased. 'I don't suppose Suze has given one thought to how Serendipity might take this. So long as her client gets her stupid show.'

'Well, you can tell Serendipity from me that I don't read the sort of trashy magazines that print this crap, and I won't be watching her mum's reality show. And I imagine a lot of people will feel the same.' Simon drank some tea. 'Now, I really had better get up and ready.' He moved towards the bathroom, then looked back at Pippa. 'Will you be OK?'

Pippa scowled. 'I'll be fine. I'm absolutely furious with Suze, though. I thought after that call on Friday night — Oh my God!'

Simon came back and sat beside her. 'What?'

'She wasn't ringing to say sorry for what she'd done, was she? She was apologising for what she was about to do!'

Simon put an arm around her. 'You don't need to comfort me,' she said. 'I'm not upset so much as furious. I'm tempted to ring her right now and give her a piece of my mind. Or better, denounce her *and* her client in the comments section of every publication she's put this rubbish in.'

'But you won't, will you?'

'No. I'll text Serendipity to let her know what's happened, and tell her not to read any of it. When I've dropped the kids off we can discuss how she wants to handle it. And until then I'm not dealing with any media enquiries.'

'Good,' said Simon, and kissed her.

***

'Don't wanna walk!' cried Ruby, as Pippa put her shoes on.

'It'll do you good,' said Pippa. 'It'll certainly do me good.'

'It could rain,' ventured Freddie.

Pippa rounded on him. 'Freddie, it's a ten-minute walk to your school, if that. You both have coats with hoods. I think we can cope with a bit of rain.' Freddie shrank back as if he'd been blasted by a gale. 'Sorry, Freddie, Mummy's a bit grumpy this morning.'

'Work stuff?'

'Yes.' She zipped up his coat for him and ruffled his hair. 'Work stuff.'

As they approached the school gate she spied a familiar curly-haired figure waiting. 'Hi, Lila. Don't you usually come in by the other gate?'

'Mmm,' said Lila. 'Could I have a word?' She looked nervous, which for Lila was almost unprecedented.

Pippa sighed. 'Why not.'

Lila watched Freddie and Bella run into the playground together before speaking. 'Is there anything I ought to know about the wedding?'

Pippa frowned. 'In what way?'

'Well, yesterday I updated my status and tagged Higginbotham Hall, and then I got this email...' She tapped at her phone and held it out to Pippa.

Dear Lila,

I do hope we shall be able to fulfil your booking in

158

December. However, as we haven't been granted a licence to hold ceremonies yet it might be wise for you to have a back-up plan...

'What does she mean?' asked Lila.

'Oh, I see!' cried Pippa. 'The inspector came out to see the Hall and she said she was happy to approve it but we needed to send her an action plan. I'm waiting for Lady H to send me the risk assessment, and then I'll do the plan, send it, and everything will be fine.'

Lila bit her lip. 'You're sure?'

'Absolutely. I'll chase it up as soon as I've dropped Ruby off, and get it sent this morning.'

'And you'll let me know?'

'Of course I'll let you know!' Pippa stuck a big grin on her face to cover the fact that now she'd like to murder Lady Higginbotham as well as Suze.

'That's all right then,' said Lila. 'I was a bit worried.'

'It's all in hand,' said Pippa.

***

Pippa's phone buzzed as she left the nursery.

Serendipity: *I've seen it. Can we talk?*

Serendipity picked up on the first ring. 'I feel so betrayed,' she said.

'It won't help, but I do too,' said Pippa. 'I would never have believed Suze would do this.'

'People are horrible sometimes,' said Serendipity. 'I know this is nothing next to all those murders that are going on, but...'

She was quiet for a few moments. Birds sang in the trees, accompanied by the faint hum of distant traffic.

'I'm just walking back from nursery,' said Pippa. 'There's one thing I must do this morning, but I can come round now and we can talk it over.'

'I'm not sure I want to talk about it at all,' said Serendipity.

'OK, what *would* you like to do?'

Serendipity said nothing.

The pavement ended and Pippa carried on walking, keeping well to the side. 'I'm sorry if that sounded a bit — angry. It's been quite a morning.'

'It's OK,' said Serendipity, in a small voice which indicated that it probably wasn't.

'I'll be with you in a few minutes, honest.' Pippa had to raise her voice over the growl of an approaching car. She looked round, and —

Her head hit the wall as she flung herself against it. Air rushed past, with a tang of petrol and metal and certain death. Blood sang in her ears.

Pippa opened her eyes to grey sky, and felt rough cold stone beneath her fingers.

The car had gone. It hadn't stopped to see if she was all right.

Her phone lay a few feet away, and she walked slowly to retrieve it. It was surprisingly hard to bend down, and harder to straighten up. The screen had cracked, but somehow Serendipity's call was still running.

That could have been me.

They might come back.

'Pippa? Pippa!' said the phone.

'A car . . . a car drove straight at me,' said Pippa, and

160

hurried down the road to where the pavement began again. In a few seconds there would be houses, and the road which led back into the village, and everything would be all right.

'*What?*' said Serendipity.

'I'm going to the police station. I'll call you.' Pippa ended the call, touching the screen gingerly, and the hand holding the phone started to shake. She stuffed the phone in her pocket before she dropped it, then after a few steps took it out and dialled Jim Horsley's number.

'Bit early for you, isn't it?' said Jim. 'And no, I haven't found out about the archive search. I do need sleep occasionally, you know.'

'Someone just tried to run me over.'

'*What?* Where are you? Are you OK?'

'I'm in the village. Are you at the police station?'

'No, at Gadcester.' A pause. 'Go somewhere with people. Oh damn, everything's closed on a Monday. Um, go to the library and stay there. I'll get to you as soon as I can.' The phone muted suddenly; Pippa guessed a hand over the microphone. 'Are you hurt?'

'Only my phone.' Pippa started to laugh, and suddenly she couldn't stop. 'I'm heading into the village,' she gasped, between giggles.

'OK. Get Norm to make you a cup of tea with lots of sugar. You sound as if you need it. I'll be there soon.'

The call ended. Pippa stared at the phone for a moment, then pocketed it and took the turn into the village. She could see people now, mums with toddlers stopping for a chat, the postman in his shorts... The lights in the library were on, and she looked both ways before running across the road and pushing open the door.

'You're an early bird,' said Norm, and then he saw the expression on her face. 'What's happened?' he asked, standing up.

'Someone tried to kill me. Jim Horsley says I have to stay here till he comes.' Pippa's knees wobbled.

Norm rushed over and helped her to a chair. 'Do you want to talk about it?'

Pippa shook her head. 'I should text Simon.'

'Shouldn't you call him?' Norm asked, gently.

'He'll — ask me things. And he'll probably be angry.' She pulled out her phone. *Nearly got hit by a car but I'm fine and safe at the library x*

'That message won't worry him in the slightest, will it?' Norm straightened up. 'I was about to make tea, would you like one?'

Pippa sighed. 'You're going to put sugar in it, aren't you?'

Norm looked slightly guilty. 'Yes.'

Pippa sighed. 'As long as I know.'

CHAPTER 19

By the time PC Horsley arrived Pippa had assured a panicked Simon that no-one would be able to ram-raid the library and if they did she would shelter in the kitchen, sent several calming messages to Serendipity, who was on the verge of hysterics, and choked down a cup of disgustingly sweet tea.

'You look pretty well for someone who's survived a murder attempt,' he said, surveying Pippa as she sat in Norm's chair at the desk.

'Is that line from the police handbook?' asked Pippa.

'No, it bloody isn't,' he replied. 'I've got the car outside and I'm taking you to the police station to make a statement.' His face was set, stern, like it had been the first few times they had met. 'Unless you have anything more pressing to do?'

Pippa opened her mouth to reply. 'I didn't think so. Come along, Norm's got a library to run.'

Norm, with a glance at the policeman, got up and

unlatched the door, and Jim Horsley ushered her out. Pippa half-expected him to produce a pair of handcuffs, or push her head down when she got into the car.

They drove the short distance to the police station in silence, apart from an occasional buzz from the police radio. 'In we go,' said Jim. He unlocked the door, held it for Pippa, then bolted it. 'Back room.'

The back room hadn't changed much since Pippa's last visit, except that the film posters had been supplemented with a couple of new ones. Jim placed a chair for Pippa, then sat behind the desk. Pippa considered asking about tea, but he didn't seem to be in the mood for social niceties.

'Right.' He clicked his pen. 'Statement from Mrs Pippa Parker, taken at nine-thirty-five on Monday the fifteenth of October 2018. Mrs Parker, please can you confirm your name and address and then, in your own words, describe exactly what happened this morning.'

Pippa began, slowly at first, and then the words tumbled out of her, until the policeman had to ask her to slow down.

'OK.' Jim looked up. 'And you didn't see the car registration?'

'No. It happened so quickly. I turned and it was almost on top of me. I only had time to jump back. It was a grey car.'

'Grey or silver?'

'Dark silver, sort of.'

'Gunmetal?'

'That's it.'

'Can you remember a badge?'

Pippa shook her head. 'I'm sorry, no.'

'Was it a small car, or a large one?'

'It was — not an SUV, and not a small car. A family car.'

'OK.' The policeman made a note. 'And it didn't stop.'

'No. It was gone by the time I'd recovered enough to look for it.'

'Mm. Is there any chance that the driver might not have seen you?'

'I don't think so.' Pippa indicated her red top.

'You said that you were talking on the phone. Could you have walked out in front of the car?' His eyes rested on Pippa, but she couldn't read their expression, and his face was neutral.

'Absolutely not,' snapped Pippa. 'I walk Ruby and Freddie down that road and I always take care on that part. I stay close to the wall.'

'The driver didn't sound the horn, or swerve?'

'I don't know if they swerved or not. They certainly didn't sound the horn.'

'We can check for tyre marks later.' The policeman paused. 'Do you have anything else that you wish to say, Mrs Parker?'

'No,' said Pippa, feeling strangely flat.

'In that case we'll finish there. Can you read through what I have written and sign it to confirm that it is an accurate statement, please.'

Pippa did as she was asked, and waited for him to speak. 'What happens now?' she ventured.

Jim Horsley leaned forward. 'I'm going to phone Gerald Tamblyn and you will give him an interview about what just happened. In that interview you will plead for drivers to be more careful on country roads. You will also say that if it *was* the QWERTY Murderer then you have no idea why he targeted you, since you are not a member of the police force and have nothing to do with the case. Then we'll go to your house and you will hand me everything to do with the case, including any notes you have made.'

'Are you going to arrest me afterwards?' said Pippa. 'You sound as if you'd like to.'

He muttered something and Pippa glared at him. 'I didn't catch that,' she said. 'Try again.'

He glared right back. 'I *said* that if locking you up would keep you safe, maybe I should.'

'Oh.' All the fight rushed out of her. 'I didn't mean to almost get run over,' she said softly.

'I should never have let you get involved.' He went to the filing cabinet, pulled the top drawer open, and rummaged, head down.

'What are you looking for?'

'Never you mind.'

Pippa walked over and touched his arm. 'I got myself involved,' she said. 'It isn't your fault, not at all.'

Jim slammed the cabinet shut and caught her up in a hug so fierce it was hard to breathe. 'I'm so sorry, Pippa,' he said into her hair.

'It's OK,' Pippa whispered, not entirely sure what was OK and what was not. The world had suddenly become very small indeed, a tight, warm cocoon of wool and strong arms around her. She could feel Jim's heart thumping next to hers, his hands holding her close. And she wasn't sure what would happen if she looked up at him. Or what she wanted to happen.

Jim sighed, the hug loosened, and he looked into her eyes, still holding her. 'No more investigating. Please.' It was less a command than an entreaty. 'I care too much about you to let you get killed.'

Pippa held his gaze. 'Do you?'

All the sternness she knew, and all his usual humour, had gone from Jim's blue eyes. 'Yes. I do.' He blinked. Then his hands moved slowly down to Pippa's, and he held them for a second before stepping back. 'So when you've quite finished messing about,' he said, very softly, 'let's get this interview over with, and then I can hand you back to your husband.'

***

Pippa and Jim, sitting on opposite sides of the dining table, both started as the doorbell rang. 'That'll be Serendipity,' said Pippa. 'Thanks for staying with me. And I hope the notes are useful.'

'Me too,' said Jim, getting up. 'The sooner we catch the QWERTY Murderer, the better I'll like it.'

Pippa could see Serendipity's slim shape through the double door. 'It's definitely her.' She opened the door to a stricken Serendipity. 'Come in. I'll get the kettle on.'

'Pippa! Are you all right?' Serendipity seemed, if anything, more distressed than Pippa.

'I'll, um, see myself out,' said Jim. 'If you think of anything else, ring the central number.' He nodded to

167

Serendipity, stepped over the threshold without a backward glance, and walked to the car, notes in hand.

'And that was that,' said Pippa, watching him go.

'What do you mean?' asked Serendipity.

Pippa sighed. 'Nothing. It doesn't matter. Let's go in.' She locked the door and led the way to the kitchen. 'Tea or coffee?'

'Tea, please. I've drunk so much coffee I'm buzzing.' Serendipity paused. 'Won't you need to fetch Ruby soon? I can come, if it helps.'

'It's OK, I've asked Sheila to do it just this once.' Pippa dropped teabags into the mugs. 'I — I couldn't face the walk to the nursery, and if someone has messed with my car...' She leaned her elbows on the worktop and put her face in her hands. 'I hope that was the end of it.'

'I feel terrible,' said Serendipity. 'If you hadn't been on the phone to me —'

'Don't be silly,' said Pippa. 'They were clearly trying to run me over. I'll — I'll just have to be a bit more careful until the police have caught whoever it is.' Her mind flipped through her weekly routine — dropping Freddie off, taking Ruby to nursery or playgroup or Sheila, picking Freddie up, going shopping, walking to the library — 'It'll be horrendous. But at least I'm not in a hospital bed, or worse.'

'And you're not — involved with the case?'

'Not any more.' The kettle pinged and Pippa sunk each teabag in turn.

'Oh.' Serendipity fetched the milk. 'How does that feel?'

'Bit early to say,' said Pippa, squeezing the teabags and flicking them into the bin. 'As if something's missing that should be there. Sort of like losing an arm. Anyway.' She poured the milk and handed a mug to Serendipity. 'Let's talk about other stuff.'

They sat awkwardly in the lounge. 'I've read the articles,' said Serendipity. 'I couldn't stop myself. At least it was a distraction from worrying about you.'

'And what did you think?' asked Pippa. Serendipity was right; discussing this was much easier than thinking of her own problems.

Serendipity shrugged. 'It was all puffed-up headlines with nothing underneath, except some family photos and stuff about the show. I thought I'd be upset, but I'm just angry.'

'Good.'

'All it basically said was that I don't get on with my family and don't see them very often. Which I'd admit myself.' Serendipity snorted.

'So what do you want to do?' asked Pippa.

Serendipity made a face. 'I don't think there's anything *to* do. I can't stop them doing their stupid show, can I?'

'Nope.'

'Then I'll ignore it and carry on as usual. Assuming that everyone doesn't cancel their bookings because they think I'm an awful person.'

'I doubt it. You'll probably get questions, so it might be as well to have a stock answer ready.' Pippa fetched her laptop and logged into the booking system for Serendipity's events. 'Ummm . . . have you got your diary

169

with you?'

'On my phone.' Serendipity pulled it out of her jeans pocket. 'Why? Is it bad? Are people cancelling?'

'They are not.' Pippa turned the screen to face Serendipity. 'You're booked solid. And there are...' She scrolled down the page. 'About two hundred new signups to your mailing list. Better get scheduling.'

A slow smile spread over Serendipity's face. 'Maybe I should donate some of the proceeds to the family roof.'

Pippa felt a smile tug at the corners of her own mouth. 'Maybe you should.'

***

Sheila delivered Ruby back to the house at two o'clock, as arranged. 'She's been a little star,' she said, as Ruby climbed over the step and went in search of the TV.

'Has she really?' asked Pippa, scrutinising her mother-in-law.

Sheila wrinkled her nose. 'She's been a little madam to be honest, but I thought you had enough on your plate. Now, are *you* all right?'

'I've had better days,' admitted Pippa. 'Would you like a cuppa? I'll get your china cup out. I've even got biscuits.' She could hear the pleading note in her voice.

'Biscuits? Then how could I refuse?'

'Mummy! The TV won't go!'

'I ought to limit your screen time, Ruby,' said Pippa, switching the television on and changing to a children's channel.

'She'll probably fall asleep in a few minutes,' said Sheila. 'She's been on the go ever since I picked her up.'

'Sorry.'

'No need to apologise.' Sheila studied Pippa. 'Now why isn't my son here with you?'

'I told him to stay at work,' said Pippa, sheepishly. 'He'd only fuss, and I'm not in the mood for fuss. I've already had to speak to the *Chronicle* about "my hit-and-run ordeal".'

'Oh dear.' Sheila looked rather amused. 'I thought you'd enjoy a bit of fuss.'

'You must be kidding. And — there's something else.'

Pippa braced herself for a cross-examination, but it didn't come. Sheila was studying her with a curious expression on her face. 'What sort of something else?' she asked, quietly.

'I've been thrown off the case. As much as I was ever on it. I've handed all my notes to Jim Horsley. I should probably take his number off my phone.' She picked it up and scrolled to *Contacts*.

'Don't.' Sheila took the phone out of her hand and put it on the worktop. 'You never know when you might need that number.'

'He probably wouldn't answer if I rang it,' said Pippa.

Sheila snorted. 'Of course he would.' Pippa looked up at that, but Sheila's face seemed entirely innocent of any dubious meaning. 'But the police can't have you running round investigating, not when someone's tried to kill you to get you off the case. Just stay low-key, and keep your eyes and ears open.'

'Yes.' Sometimes Pippa wondered if Sheila thought they were in a TV show.

'The killer's running scared now,' said Sheila dreamily. 'They're bound to slip up.'

'I hope so,' said Pippa. She peeked into the lounge, where Ruby, as predicted, was curled up fast asleep on the sofa. 'But without notes, or any information from the police, all I can do is get on with my own stuff and wait.'

'Then that's what you do,' said Sheila. 'Ready to spring when the time comes.'

'Of course,' said Pippa. 'Ready to spring, that's me.' In reality she didn't think she had ever felt less springy, but it was nice that someone else thought she was a finely-tuned menace to criminals. Even if it was her mother-in-law.

CHAPTER 20

Pippa jumped at the sound of a key in the front door. *Of course it's Simon*, she told herself. *Don't be ridiculous.* She walked into the hall. 'You're early.'

'I was in early,' said Simon. He looked at her searchingly, then crossed the hall and gave her a gentle hug. 'How are you?'

'I'm OK,' Pippa said into his shoulder. 'I've been minded until I could take no more. Tea with sugar in, and everything.'

'Good.' He released her, and that searching look was there again. 'I could have got out of that meeting, you know.'

Pippa sighed. 'You'd have rushed home and asked me questions and mollycoddled me.'

'Would that have been so bad?'

'Don't be silly.' Pippa pushed her hair back. 'Anyway, you're just in time to walk to school with us and pick up Freddie.'

'I thought I would be.' Simon beckoned her into the corner furthest from the lounge, where Ruby was still dozing. 'What on earth do we do?' he whispered. 'Do we move somewhere else, or take taxis everywhere, or what?'

'You don't need to worry,' said Pippa. 'I've given an interview to the *Chronicle* and said I'm not working on the case and have nothing to do with it. And I've handed everything to J — PC Horsley. That should be enough to reassure the murderer that I'm no threat.'

'I hope they believe you,' said Simon.

'I hope the police catch them,' said Pippa.

'Wait a minute.' Simon frowned. 'Did Jim Horsley bring you home?'

'Yes,' said Pippa. 'He took a statement, made me do an interview with the *Chronicle*, brought me home, took my notes, and then Serendipity arrived.'

'Oh. OK.' Simon loosened his tie. 'I just —'

'You've really got nothing to worry about, since I doubt I'll ever work with him again,' snapped Pippa. 'And now I'm going to be late. Thanks very much for your help.' She grabbed her keys from the hall table and left, barely remembering not to slam the door.

There were no dangerous roads between her house and the school, but still Pippa kept an eye out, for largish grey cars in particular. Her heart skipped a beat as she turned the corner and saw one — but it was parked and no one was inside. She took a picture of it on her phone, just in case.

Miss Darcy's door was opening as Pippa hurried into the playground. Lila spied her and waved. 'Pippa! Did you do the thing?'

Pippa sighed. 'Not yet. Someone tried to kill me this morning, so I've been unexpectedly busy.'

'What?!'

'Yup. I'll send another reminder now.' She pulled out her phone with half an eye on the door. *PLEASE can you send me the fire risk doc? I can't do a plan without it and time's running out! Pippa.* She showed it to Lila, then pressed *Send*.

'Never mind that,' said Lila. 'What do you mean, someone tried to kill you?'

'Nearly got run over on the way back from nursery,' said Pippa. 'They didn't stop. I've told the police.' She stopped talking as Mrs Ridout appeared, peering into the playground to try and match each child to its parent.

'Maybe it wouldn't be such a bad thing if we did postpone it,' said Lila. 'We can't agree on anything. We don't even like the same flowers.' She laughed, but it was a brittle sound with no amusement in it.

'Does any of that matter?' A couple of parents turned to look, but Pippa didn't care. 'So long as you love each other and actually want to get married?'

Lila opened her mouth and closed it again.

'Quite honestly, if the pair of you really can't make a decision then you may as well let Bella choose. At least you'd get somewhere then.' Out of the corner of her eye Pippa saw Mrs Ridout waving, Freddie beside her. She waved back and Freddie ran over. 'Anyway. Let me know when you've decided what you want. I've got too much on my mind right now to waste time debating whether

175

flamingoes would look better than parrots. Come along, Freddie.'

'Where's Ruby?' asked Freddie.

'With Daddy, at home.' Pippa held out her hand, he slipped his hot little one into it, and she felt oddly comforted as they walked to the school gate. 'Let's go and have a treat at the tearoom together.' She texted Simon to let him know, and set off. If the murderer was waiting to ambush her, they'd have to hang around a bit longer.

***

'Pippa! Wait!'

Pippa turned. Lila, towing Bella, was in hot pursuit, curls bobbing.

She sighed and stopped. 'If this is about flamingoes —'

'Don't be ridiculous,' panted Lila. 'Come and have a coffee with me.'

'We're going to the tearoom,' said Pippa. 'You can join us if you like.'

'Are you sure you're all right?' Lila put a hand on her arm.

'*Yes*,' said Pippa, pulling away.

'You clearly aren't. Right, you're coming to mine.'

'What about the tearoom?' whined Freddie.

'I've got doughnuts,' said Lila, which worked like a charm.

'It seems a long time since I've been round,' said Pippa, as Lila opened the door.

'Not since school started,' said Lila. She busied herself making squash and putting doughnuts on plates. 'You two can have TV rights, provided you behave. Understood?'

Freddie and Bella nodded in unison and scampered into the lounge. Lila sighed and followed them with the squash and doughnuts.

In her absence Pippa filled the kettle and switched it on, then rooted in the cupboards for mugs. There were a few more now that Jeff had moved in, mostly with the logo of his bank on them, but one large *Star Wars* one. There were also a lot more teaspoons in the drawer.

'I've put *Wreck-It Ralph* on for them,' said Lila as she returned. 'That should hold them for at least an hour.' Her eyes narrowed. 'Sit at the breakfast bar,' she said. 'You look wobbly.'

'I feel wobbly,' said Pippa, doing as she was told.

'I'm not surprised. Tea or coffee?'

'Tea, please.'

'Normal or decaf?' Pippa raised her eyebrows. 'I know, blame Jeff.'

Pippa sighed. 'Probably decaf. I don't think I need any more stimulation at the moment.'

Lila didn't say any more until the tea was made. 'I think this is the decaf one,' she said, setting a mug in front of Pippa. 'Do you want to tell me about it?'

'Not particularly.' Pippa sipped her tea, met Lila's watchful eyes, and sighed. 'I'm sorry I was snappy about the flamingoes.'

Lila sniggered. 'You're obsessed with those flamingoes!' She drank from her own cup, muttered 'Knew it,' and switched the two mugs round. Then she ran her fingers through her curls. 'It's just — I want it to be really special. And I worry that if Jeff and I can't even

177

compromise on silly things like table decorations, what will we do when something big happens?'

'Maybe that's why you're squabbling,' said Pippa. 'Because it doesn't matter.'

'I hope so,' said Lila into her cup. 'I wish it felt more — stable. Like you and Simon.'

Pippa stared at her, then burst into tears. Soon Lila's arm was around her. 'I'm sorry, Pippa, what did I say?'

'Nothing,' Pippa squeaked. Lila held her until her shoulders had stopped shaking, then handed her the kitchen roll. 'Thanks. Sorry.'

'It's OK.' Lila was looking at her curiously.

'I don't know what I think myself,' admitted Pippa, trying her tea. It tasted much the same.

Still that odd, wary look. 'About what?'

'If I tell you, this goes no further. Promise?'

Lila nodded. 'Promise.'

'If you thought that someone — liked you, and then it turned out that they did, but because you were married they would never do anything about it, would you be sad? Even though you'd never do anything about it either, because of being married?'

Lila considered for quite some time. 'Do you like the person too?' she asked, eventually.

'More than I should,' admitted Pippa, revolving her mug on its coaster.

'Yes,' said Lila. 'I would be sad.'

'I didn't mean to,' said Pippa. 'It just happened.' She pulled out her phone and opened the contacts. There he was, under *Piglet*. Her thumb hovered over *Delete Contact*.

But what if — She sighed, rubbed away a tear, and clicked on *Edit*. *Piglet* disappeared, letter by letter, and in its place she typed *PC Horsley*.

The phone shrilled, and she nearly dropped it. *Simon*.

'Pippa, where are you?' He sounded as if he were about to burst into tears.

Oh no. 'I'm at Lila's. Sorry, I —'

'Are you all right? Tell me you're all right! I took Ruby to the tearoom and you weren't there, and I thought — Is Freddie with you?'

'Yes, Freddie's here.' She sniffed. 'I — I'm sorry.'

'I'm coming over,' said Simon. 'I want to be sure you're OK. I should have come home when you texted this morning.'

'OK,' said Pippa, in a small voice.

Lila got another mug from the cupboard. 'Emotional reunion?' she asked, under her breath.

Pippa's mouth twitched, and she nodded.

Lila smiled. 'Good.'

***

They were still there when Jeff came in from work, bundled up on the sofa watching *The Incredibles*. 'Long time no see,' he commented, shaking hands with Simon.

'I thought we could ring for pizza,' said Lila.

'Gosh,' said Jeff. 'A dinner party, on a Monday.'

Pippa squeezed Simon's hand. 'Maybe we should make it a wedding planning party.'

'That's an idea,' said Jeff. 'Simon can act as referee.'

Pippa's phone buzzed in her pocket. She thought about ignoring it. *That won't do any good.*

179

Lady H: *I don't understand, Pippa, I sent the plan to you when you first asked, on Wednesday. June Higginbotham x*

'You really didn't,' Pippa told the phone, then looked in her mailbox to make sure. 'Nope.'

Unless...

'Oh for heaven's sake.' There it was, in the junk mail folder. *Fire risk assessment*, with a paperclip.

'All OK?' asked Simon, hugging her a little more tightly.

Pippa sighed and put her head on his shoulder. 'Yes,' she said, a couple of seconds later. 'All OK.'

CHAPTER 21

Pippa needn't have worried about walking to school alone but for the children the next day. Firstly, Lila called round for her; secondly, on the way to school and in the playground she was accosted by every parent whom she had nodding acquaintance with, plus many she didn't know at all.

'I saw you in the paper this morning!'

'Do you really think it was the QWERTY —' a swift glance at Freddie — 'you-know-who?'

'Did they send a journalist round to interview you?'

Pippa managed smiles and yeses and nos in the right places before Lila whisked her into a tight group with Imogen, Caitlin and Sam. 'At this rate you should get your own PR,' she grumbled.

'I wish they'd used a nicer photo,' said Pippa. 'It's always the one from the festival where I'm holding a clipboard and pointing.'

'Authoritative, you see,' said Imogen. 'Even bossy

people are at risk.'

'Thanks.'

The reception classroom door opened and Miss Darcy herself appeared. 'Everyone in, please,' she said. 'Don't bother lining up today. Freddie, come *along*.' She gave Pippa a disapproving look.

'One hundred lines,' said Lila. 'I must not wind up the QWERTY Murderer.'

'Maybe it was Miss Darcy,' said Caitlin. 'She's had enough of your persistent slacking, Pippa.'

'How dare you,' said Pippa. 'I've even done Freddie's form for the trip. And paid.'

'Oh darn,' said Sam, frowning. 'I knew there was something. I'll go through Livvy's bag tonight.'

Miss Darcy counted the children in and disappeared from view. Mrs Ridout came to the door, presumably watching for stragglers. A parent drifted over, her eye on Pippa.

'Question approaching at one o'clock,' said Caitlin. 'Let's get out of here.'

Pippa opened playgroup with a statement. 'I bet most of you are dying to ask me about what was in the paper this morning. Yes it did happen, yes I think it was that person, no I'm not working on the case, and I have no idea who did it. And that's all I have to say on the matter.' She went to fill the urn and steal a biscuit feeling considerably better.

The downside was that, apart from a few questions on housekeeping matters, no one talked to her. Caitlin was busy with Josh, who was having a clingy day, and Pippa spent much of the session either getting Ruby out of heated disputes over the play kitchen or reading the fire risk assessment for Higginbotham Hall on her phone. *The fun never stops*, she thought wearily.

'Are you really off the case, dear?' were Sheila's first words to her when she went to drop Ruby off.

'Yup,' said Pippa. 'Mind like a blank sheet of paper, that's me.'

Sheila looked suspicious.

'I'm honestly not bluffing,' said Pippa. 'There is no cunning plan.'

'If you say so, dear,' said Sheila, and shut the door.

Pippa got into the Mini and drove home, testing her brakes every so often on the way. So far, all seemed fine. Perhaps she wasn't of any interest to the QWERTY Murderer now that she had given up the case. The thought gave her a little pang. She imagined Inspector Fanshawe and PC Gannet and — yes, Jim Horsley, bent over a map in Gadcester Police Station, or talking through statements together, stabbing fingers at relevant words —

She focused on a red light just in time and braked hurriedly.

Back at home Pippa double-locked the door, checked the windows, then sat down at the laptop and composed an action plan for the fire risk assessment, including costings for signage and modifying a couple of doors. She read through it to check she had covered the things Daisy Franks had mentioned, then emailed it to Lady Higginbotham and texted her to say it had arrived.

She sighed with relief, then checked her watch. Still only 1.45. Lots of time until pickup. She switched to the browser and typed *Gadcester Chron* —

No. I'll ring Serendipity. That's what I should be doing, checking up on my clients.

'Pippa!' Serendipity exclaimed.

'At last, someone who's pleased to hear from me,' said Pippa.

'Oh,' said Serendipity. 'You might not be so happy when I tell you why I'm pleased.'

Pippa sighed. 'Go on, hit me.'

'Well,' said Serendipity, 'I've um, had a few phone calls. Look, would it be easier if I came over? Then I can play you the messages.'

'Yes, why not,' said Pippa.

The doorbell rang a few minutes later, which was quick for Serendipity. *It must be good news*, thought Pippa, getting up. *And I need some of that.*

'So what won't I be happy about?', she said to Serendipity's beaming face.

Monty barked and wagged his tail. 'Come on Monty, into the garden with you,' said Serendipity briskly. 'If that's all right, of course, Pippa.'

'Oh yes,' said Pippa, watching Serendipity march through the house and let Monty out. *What's come over her?*

'So,' said Serendipity as Pippa switched the kettle on, 'I had my phone on silent, because, you know, Mummy and your horrible friend, and when I checked it there were a couple of voicemails. At first I thought I should delete them, in case they were trolls. But then I thought, who would have my number?'

'So you listened,' said Pippa. 'And?'

'And it was the production company who are doing Mummy's show.'

'Not again,' said Pippa.

'No,' said Serendipity, leaning forward. 'They asked if I'd consider making a pilot for a crafting show, and that they'd send an email with the concept. And the other message was them ringing back and asking me to check my email. So of course I did. And when I did —'

'There was more than one?'

'There was that one. And there was one from my publisher to say they're doubling my print run. And *then* —' Serendipity paused, clearly for dramatic effect, 'there was one from the guest booker on *Weekday Morning*, asking if I could come in on Friday and do a fifteen-minute slot on scones.'

Pippa gripped the worktop. 'No *way.*'

'Yes way.' Serendipity got two mugs from the cupboard. 'So I'll need you to do lots of work for me.'

'That's . . . wonderful,' said Pippa, slowly.

'Isn't it?' said Serendipity. 'More events, more signings, more bookings...'

'More everything,' said Pippa. 'But I also think . . . more staff.'

'How do you mean?' asked Serendipity.

'I mean,' said Pippa, 'that you should get a proper manager or agent-type person who can negotiate all this, for starters. I can organise you, but this is specialist stuff. TV work, more books maybe, national-level press. Who knows, maybe even merchandise.'

'Gosh,' said Serendipity. 'I see your point.'

'I don't suppose anyone like that has landed in your inbox?' asked Pippa.

'Not yet,' said Serendipity. 'The one thing I do know is that it won't be your friend. She may have the contacts, but I couldn't trust her.'

'That,' said Pippa, 'is absolutely fine by me.'

***

'Good day?' asked Simon, as they sat together on the sofa, watching a cookery show.

'Yeah,' said Pippa. 'I'm glad Lady H's stuff is finally done. Another box ticked. And I'm really pleased for Serendipity.' *And I've stayed out of trouble for a whole day*, she added to herself.

'That is brilliant.' Simon stroked her knee. 'All thanks to you, of course.'

Pippa shrugged. 'Oh, I just asked a few questions. Once Serendipity thought of some people with the sort of profile she wants, it was easy to find out who their management were.'

'Yes, but she wouldn't have got there — and certainly not to having a couple of meetings set up — without your help.' The stroking continued. 'You are very smart, Pip.'

'All right, what do you want?'

'That's a bit harsh!' Simon laughed. 'But yes, I do need to ask you something.'

'Here we go.' Pippa rolled her eyes.

'Well . . . could Declan come for supper one evening this week?'

'If he can bear my cooking, sure,' said Pippa. 'Any

reason?'

'He's got ideas,' said Simon, 'about the merger-takeover-whatever it is. We both have. And it would be easier to talk them through in a place where we aren't worrying about being found out.'

'You make it sound like you're having an affair,' said Pippa.

'I know,' said Simon. 'Like that time someone tipped me off about you sneaking to the police station.'

'Fair point,' said Pippa, feeling a little raw. 'Yes, fine. Let me know what day, and if there's anything he doesn't eat.' She paused. 'You would tell me if there was trouble at work, wouldn't you?'

'Course I would,' said Simon. 'It just feels silly having to be secretive about talking to someone who could be a lot of help.'

'Yes,' said Pippa. 'If only Suze had talked to me, instead of going behind my back, maybe she'd be managing Serendipity now.' Something tugged at her brain — a reminder of someone else. Who was she thinking of?

'Great, I'll text him,' said Simon, taking his arm from round Pippa.

'Eager beaver,' said Pippa absently. *Who was it? Someone sneaky...*

'How's Thursday? Say supper for 8pm?'

'No problem.' *Who else has gone behind my back?*

'He says he eats everything.'

'All right, how about roast chicken?'

'Lovely.' Simon's thumbs flew over the keys, then his

187

phone beeped. 'That's a yes.'

'I'll shop tomorrow,' said Pippa.

'Great, all set.' Simon put his phone on the coffee table. 'And thank you, this will really help. You know what they say, two heads are better than one.'

Pippa stabbed a triumphant finger in the air. 'That's it! Janey Dixon!'

Simon gawped at her. 'What's Janey Dixon?'

'The other person I was trying to think of who double-crossed me!'

Simon looked puzzled. 'Does that matter? Are you worried that someone, possibly either you or Serendipity, is planning to bump Suze off?'

'Yeah,' said Pippa, grinning. 'We'll team up and do a pincer movement on her — Oh my God.' She stared at Simon. 'That's it.'

'*What's* it, Pip? You're making even less sense than usual.'

'I've got it. I know why the QWERTY Murderer did the ABC thing.'

'But you knew that anyway. To make everyone think of the Agatha Christie book.'

'That was part of it. But it wasn't the main reason.'

'I give up,' said Simon, shaking his head. 'Are you going to tell me or not?'

'Not yet,' replied Pippa, picking up her own phone. 'I need to think it through first. And as you just said, two heads are better than one.'

CHAPTER 22

'Pick up, come on, pick up,' Pippa muttered into the ringing phone. 'What's taking him so long?'

'Maybe he's busy,' said Simon.

'Huh,' said Pippa. 'Priorities.'

At last the phone clicked. 'Um, hello,' said Jim Horsley.

'It's me, Pippa.'

'Yes, I know that.'

'I think I've got it.'

'Who is it, Jim?' Mandy's voice, somewhere in the background.

'I won't be long,' he called back. His voice dropped to a mutter. 'Pippa, what did we agree about you not working on this case any more?'

'Yes I know, but Simon and I were discussing work stuff, and it set off something in my brain, and —'

'It's her, isn't it?' Mandy's voice again, louder. 'It's that bloody Pippa Parker woman!'

The phone muffled for a few moments, then cleared.

'Would you mind if I put you on speakerphone?' asked Jim.

'Fine by me,' said Pippa, trying to keep the note of glee out of her voice and failing completely.

'OK, hang on.' She could hear fumbling. 'Carry on.'

'The reason why we keep coming to a dead end is because there isn't any logic linking Janey's murder and Ritz's attempted murder, except for them working in the same building. The only way you can link them to one person is to assume that it's a serial killer with some sort of weird obsession.'

'Yes, and…' Jim sounded rather fatigued.

'What if we weren't dealing with one murderer, but two?'

Silence on the other end of the line. Then Jim and Mandy said in unison. 'Go on.'

***

'Please stop dashing about,' said Simon, watching Pippa stuff extra nappies into the changing bag.

'Can't help it,' said Pippa.

'I know.'

She stopped, stared at Simon, then came over and kissed him. 'Thanks for agreeing to do the drop-off this morning. And booking the extra session.'

'You don't have to thank me. They're my kids too.'

'Yes, but —' She kissed him again. 'Thanks anyway.'

'You can thank me properly later,' he said, with a very obvious wink.

Pippa made a face. 'Not if you do that I won't. Anyway, got to go.'

'Have you said goodbye to the kids?'

'Yup. I don't think they were awake, though. Maybe give them an extra kiss from me.'

'On it. Now go and fight crime.'

Pippa let herself out of the house, looking all around for lurkers, and got into the Mini. The only traffic at this time was Gerry's milk float, whirring down the cul-de-sac. Pippa waved, and he waved back. She tried her brakes before turning into the main road, but they seemed fine, and soon she was on the road to Gadcester.

In the end, her phone call to Jim Horsley had lasted for about ten minutes. 'We need to have this conversation with the paperwork to hand,' he had said. 'We need the statement transcripts, and more information from Gerald and Brendan, or at least their HR team.'

Pippa sighed. 'It's so frustrating.'

'Welcome to the police force,' said Mandy.

'I'm going to ring Henry,' said Jim Horsley.

'Who's Henry?' asked Pippa.

'Sorry, Inspector Fanshawe I mean.'

'On first name terms, are we?' asked Mandy, and Pippa could detect a definite edge to her voice.

'Occasionally, off duty,' said Jim, sounding a little defensive. 'Leaving that aside, we need to get on to this first thing tomorrow. Pippa, can you come to Gadcester?'

Pippa looked at Simon. 'Can I?'

'It's a nursery day, isn't it?' said Simon. 'Yes, I can cover that and school. Do you want me to see if I can book Rubes in for the afternoon, too?'

'That's a yes, then, until school pick-up,' said Pippa.

'Although I may subsequently be murdered by a furious toddler.'

'We'll take the chance,' said Jim. 'I'll get off now, and text you with arrangements.'

Pippa slowed as she reached the street where Gadcester Police Station stood in all its looming Victorian glory. *Past the main car park*, Jim Horsley had said. *Take the alley on the right...*

There it was. Pippa signalled, and pulled into an alley with two high walls either side which seemed certain to finish in a dead end. *Please don't make me have to back out of here...*

The alley opened out on the right-hand side to show a high iron gate. A small car park was visible through the wrought-iron curlicues. On the gatepost was a button with a speaker. Pippa pressed it.

'Name please,' the speaker crackled.

'Pippa Parker.'

A pause. 'Who are you here to see?'

'Inspector Fanshawe.' Pippa was tempted to say 'Henry,' but suspected that wouldn't go down well.

The speaker buzzed, and the gate whined open. Pippa drove in and parked next to a shiny black Bentley. The car park was bristling with CCTV cameras, which, oddly, made her feel more rather than less apprehensive.

The modern glass porch at the back of the police station, while presumably more exclusive than the front, felt tacked on to the gothic stonework. A uniformed officer was on reception. 'Mrs Parker?' he said, looking down his list.

'That's me,' said Pippa.

'Please take a seat.' He picked up the phone on his desk, punched in a number, and had a short conversation. 'Someone will be with you directly.'

This reception was nothing like the main one, which was cavernous and plastered with Crimestoppers posters. It was small and plain, in a way that suggested people directed here wouldn't have to wait long. And indeed, Pippa had barely had time to draw that conclusion before a plain wood door at the back opened silently and Jim Horsley stuck his head round it. 'Come this way.'

Pippa expected to be led down the usual corridor, to the usual room, but instead Jim Horsley opened a door directly opposite the reception. 'Quieter here,' he said.

'Ah, Pippa, glad you could make it,' said Inspector Fanshawe, getting up and coming round the large table to shake her hand. 'You've stirred things up nicely.'

'Is that good?' asked Pippa, taking the seat he indicated.

'If it gets us the collar without more incidents, then yes.' Inspector Fanshawe didn't sit down, but walked over to a whiteboard on which were two lists. 'These are the employees based at the main building. Jim has begun to mark off everyone with an alibi for any one of the murders or attempted murders which have occurred.' He pointed at the board. 'For example, Gerald Tamblyn was with friends at the time when Janey Dixon was murdered, so he has a blue star by his name. However, when Ritz Robertson's car was tampered with, we only have his word for it that he was asleep in bed — so no red star.'

'I see.' Pippa gazed at the board. 'So the green star is for Sean Davies. And the purple is me.'

'I'm afraid so,' said Jim. 'The difficulty with the last two incidents is that with the building closed, unless people were actually on air or in a meeting or interview, there's little chance of an alibi. Basically those could have been almost anyone.'

Mandy came into the room bearing a tray with four mugs. 'Brews up.' She eyed Pippa. 'Morning. I was told tea no sugar.' Police uniform, it turned out, suited her better than her own clothes.

'That's just right,' said Pippa. 'Thank you.'

'I'd make Jim do it,' she replied, 'but his coffee's disgusting.' She grinned at Jim Horsley, who rolled his eyes in return.

'So would I be right in thinking,' said Pippa, 'that the newspaper people who had a watertight alibi for Janey's murder are *more* likely to be involved in this? And the other way round for the radio station people?'

'Like a swap?' asked Mandy. 'You do my dirty work if I do yours?'

'That makes sense,' said the inspector. 'But who?'

'Let's look at the people with the strongest alibis,' said Jim Horsley, drawing circles round a few names.

'That's interesting,' said Pippa. 'Did you get any leads on Sean Davies? Any sightings of joggers with coshes?'

'There was something,' said Inspector Fanshawe, opening a laptop. 'Let me do a search.' He typed, then scrolled, then turned the screen outwards. 'Here.' He pointed.

Transcript of phone call from member of the public:
'I'm ringing in because I think I saw Sean Davies at 7.05
am. He was wearing clothes like in the description and
jogging along the canal path, chatting to another jogger.
The other jogger had a beanie hat and a blue tracksuit on.
I remember thinking he must be warm in that.'

[In response to question about appearance of jogger]:
'I couldn't see much of him. His hat was over his hair. He
had dark eyebrows and no beard or moustache. Middle-
aged, I think. He was sort of medium height. I couldn't say
if he was fat or thin cos it was a baggy tracksuit. He must
have been quite fit, though, to run and talk at the same
time. They were just jogging and chatting. It might not
even have been the man who was murdered. I only saw
them for a few seconds. My dog ran off into the bushes and
I had to go after him.'

'Dark-haired, medium height, male, middle-aged...'
Mandy picked up another marker and began to draw dotted
lines round more names. 'That doesn't match any of the
newspaper staff.'

'Does anyone own a biggish dark grey car? Or have one
in the family?'

'We drew a blank on that, didn't we?' said Inspector
Fanshawe.

'We did,' said Jim Horsley. 'They could have borrowed
it from someone, but how we'd track that down...'

'Could there be more than two people involved?' asked
Mandy. 'A sort of collective?'

'I don't even want to think about that possibility,' said
the inspector. 'And the more people are involved, the more

likely it is that someone will slip up.'

'Hmmm,' said Pippa.

'That was a very significant hmmm,' said Jim Horsley. Care to share?'

'It's probably nothing,' said Pippa. 'You remember that someone tried to frame me for borrowing *The ABC Murders* and not returning it?'

Mandy snorted. 'It's hardly the same league.'

Pippa raised her eyebrows. 'I'm not saying that it is. But the only person who has a reason to do that is one of the murderers. And to do it, and write in Norm's ledger, they must have been in the library.'

'You're right.' Jim checked his watch. 'I'll ring Norm now and get him to come in. I'm afraid the voracious readers of Much Gadding may have to do without the library this morning.'

'Well, that's a lead,' said Mandy, looking at Pippa with grudging respect. 'But we still have a group of suspects and nothing much to link any two of them. All we can say for sure is that one works at the paper and one at the radio station. No prints, no DNA, and nothing in the way of clues except what the murderer or murderers have planted to send us off track.'

'When I went undercover as a cleaner, I heard some conversations,' said Pippa. 'At the time we were thinking in terms of one person, so I'm wondering if I missed something... Do you have my statement on there?' she asked the inspector.

'Should do.' The inspector typed and frowned at the screen. 'Got it.' He scrolled rapidly. 'Useful background,

196

but nothing there that could convict anyone.'

'In that case,' said Pippa, 'I have an idea.'

CHAPTER 23

'I don't suppose I can talk you out of this, can I?' asked Simon, as Pippa pulled her polo shirt over her stab vest.

'You must be kidding,' said Pippa. 'I can't wait to see if I'm right. Anyway, a day off work is a great opportunity for you. You can get on with preparing Declan's roast chicken for later.'

'I hope you get to enjoy it,' said Simon, handing Pippa her tabard.

'Not *again*, Mummy,' said Freddie, when Pippa went in to kiss him goodbye. 'Why are you wearing a thingy? Are you working at preschool?'

'Close, but not quite right,' said Pippa. 'I'll be back in time to pick you up from school, never fear. And you love going to school with Daddy.'

'He walks too fast,' grumbled Freddie.

Ruby was sitting in the corner of her cot-bed, flicking through the book Pippa had bought her. She looked up suspiciously. 'Nursery?'

'No,' said Pippa. 'Playgroup, with Daddy.'

'Oh.' Her face fell.

'Never mind,' said Pippa, kissing her. 'I'll be back as soon as I can.'

'Soon you'll know the way to Gadcester all on your own,' she told the Mini, as they bowled along the road together. 'No special car park for you today though, you'll have to put up with the other cars.'

She parked in the car park she had used the last time she had gone undercover, put her black-framed glasses on, and made her way to the newspaper offices, tugging her cap down as she did so.

'Morning,' she said as she came through the door.

Diane was sitting reading a magazine and filing her nails as if she had never left. 'Morning,' she said. 'Jodie off again?'

'Been reassigned,' said Pippa, filling in the visitors' book. 'Didn't know you'd be back so soon.'

'*We* didn't,' said Diane. 'Only got a phone call yesterday afternoon. For all they knew, I might have upped and got a job somewhere else.' She slapped the cupboard key into Pippa's palm.

'Yeah,' said Pippa.

An attempt had been made to decorate the boardroom. A small banner saying *Welcome back!* was taped to the cupboards, and confetti spread on the table. 'Bless,' said Pippa. At least it meant there was no point in even attempting to clean, beyond dusting the windowsills. She did that, then set an alarm on her phone for 8.55. That was her cue to switch on the vacuum. She wanted to look down at the street to see who was coming into the building, but didn't dare. So she folded her arms, leaned against the cabinet, and twitched.

Inspector Fanshawe materialised as she was steering the vacuum towards the door. 'Good morning,' he said. 'Don't mind us, just about to have a meeting.' Jim Horsley came in next, then Mandy. Her eyes flicked over Pippa with a hint of amusement, but she said nothing. Pippa unplugged the vacuum, coiled the flex, and settled behind her trolley in the corner, trying not to seethe.

Gerald Tamblyn was first to arrive. His glance slid past Pippa and her trolley until it found the inspector. 'This isn't exactly how I planned our return,' he said fretfully, walking towards him. 'I was hoping we could get on with our jobs and forget it all.'

'That would be nice, wouldn't it,' observed the inspector. 'Are the others on their way up?'

'They are,' said the editor.

The reporters arrived next, in a huddle; then Diane from reception, puffing a little; then the station staff. 'Ritz and Stewart will be up in a minute,' said Tony. 'They're sorting out the handover.'

Brendan Shirrell came in next, smooth and unruffled. 'Good morning, officers.' He eyed Gerald Tamblyn, and took up a position midway between the police officers at the front and the staff at the back of the room.

The lift pinged, and Ritz and Stewart, both holding *Gadcester FM* mugs, hurried in. Ritz was wearing a sky-blue neck brace which clashed with his Hawaiian shirt. 'Phil will be up in a minute,' said Stewart.

200

'All right,' said Inspector Fanshawe. 'We don't intend to stay long. We're here to welcome you back to your building and suggest a few precautions before letting you carry on as normal.'

A ripple of relief ran through the crowd. Phil entered quietly and walked towards Ritz, giving him a thumbs-up as he did so.

'So, first of all, welcome back!' Inspector Fanshawe spread his hands. 'We've concluded the part of our investigation which relates to this building, and —'

A loud cough came from where Ritz Robertson was standing. He tried to drink from his mug, but spluttered it out in another cough. The mug tipped, spilling liquid on the floor.

'Steady on, old man,' said Stewart Burgess, and thumped him on the back.

'I'll get a glass of water,' said Diane, and left the room.

Ritz continued to cough, going redder and redder. Phil took his arm and helped him to a chair, putting the mug on the table. 'Are you all right, mate?'

'Can't . . . breathe…' wheezed Ritz, between coughs.

'I'm calling 999,' said Brendan, and took out his phone.

'Wait…' Ritz choked out. Slowly his coughing eased, and the purple colour in his face began to fade. 'Sorry,' he muttered. 'Tea . . . went down the wrong way. As you were.' He leaned back in the chair, with a final cough. 'Whew.'

'As I was saying,' continued the inspector, giving Ritz a hard stare. 'We have finished investigating in this building —'

'Does that mean you've caught the QWERTY Murderer?' asked Gerald Tamblyn.

Diane returned with a plastic cup of water. 'Oh,' she said. She put the cup in front of Ritz, and stepped back to stand beside Brendan.

'Not quite,' said the inspector. 'But we're very close.'

'That isn't good enough!' exclaimed the editor. 'I'm not prepared to come to work every day knowing that my life is potentially in jeopardy! There's a crazy serial killer out there, man, and you invite us back to get picked off one by one!'

'I know you're concerned for your staff, Mr Tamblyn,' said the inspector. 'However, there's really nothing to worry about.'

'I disagree,' said Brendan. 'I'm not prepared to move my staff back into this building if this killer is at large.'

'There isn't a killer,' said PC Horsley. 'There are two. And now we know who they are.'

'What?' Gerald Tamblyn was almost as puce as Ritz had been. 'Explain yourself!'

'Gladly.' Jim Horsley had to raise his voice to make himself heard above the din which had broken out. 'I will, however, ask you to move away from the door first.' The crowd parted, and he strode to the door, turning the interior lock. 'Good.' The crowd shuffled back, but Pippa noticed that each person was holding themselves a little apart from their neighbours, and keeping their eyes firmly on the police officers.

'I'm sure you'll remember the first murder,' said Inspector Fanshawe. 'Janey Dixon, stabbed in the back with a newspaper spike. Luckily for us, the time of the attack was easy to pinpoint as she had managed to phone a member of the public, Mrs Pippa Parker.' He caught Pippa's eye. 'Pippa, would you like to join us?'

'Of course.' Pippa took off her glasses and cap, shook out her hair, and stepped from behind her trolley. She heard a whistle, coming from roughly where Gerald Tamblyn was standing, and low murmurs as she moved to join the police officers. When she faced the room, all eyes were on her. Diane looked aggrieved, Ritz and Gerald Tamblyn amused, but everyone else seemed puzzled.

'Unfortunately it was too late to save Janey,' said the inspector. 'Her injuries were too severe. The next victim, Ritz Robertson, managed to escape with superficial injuries after his brakes were tampered with.'

'Superior driving skills,' said Ritz, beaming, and appearing quite recovered.

'The difficulty for us,' said the inspector, 'was that the newspaper staff all had alibis on the night Janey Dixon was killed, and Ritz's car was tampered with in the early morning, when it was dark. But the two incidents had to be connected, because a letter A had been placed with Janey, and a letter B was found in the glove compartment of Ritz's car.'

'I jumped to the conclusion that the killer was either copying or referencing *The ABC Murders*,' said Pippa. 'But when I read the book, they obviously weren't. And when I tried to get the book from the local library, the librarian told me I'd borrowed it.'

'Curiouser and curiouser,' said the inspector. 'So we

decided to close the building, as you know, and called you in. And Mrs Parker here did some observation while she was cleaning.'

'I *knew* you were going about it all wrong,' said Diane, 'but I'm too polite to pick people up when they're making mistakes.'

'You're too kind,' said Pippa. 'I listened in on a few conversations, but heard nothing incriminating.'

'And then Sean Davies was killed,' said Jim Horsley, 'and we found an empty tube of vitamin C tablets in his pocket. The QWERTY Murderer again.'

'Meanwhile,' said Pippa, 'the murderer had worked out that I was helping the police, and tried to run me over as I walked back from my daughter's nursery. A dark grey car, fairly large. Luckily for me, I managed to jump out of the way in time. The car didn't stop, and I suspect if I had died or been seriously injured at the scene, a letter D would have been planted on me. As it was, I was removed from the case.'

'Well, so far this is a catalogue of blunder after blunder,' said Gerald Tamblyn.

'Thank you,' said the inspector. 'I hope you're following.'

'To resume,' said Jim Horsley, 'Mrs Parker had deduced that the *ABC Murders* link was a giant red herring, but we couldn't work out what the purpose was. We also couldn't find a consistent motive for the killings. C and D were committed to stop people from delving too closely into the case, since Sean Davies had announced his intention to do some investigating of his own. Pippa's involvement was obvious, and she had ignored the murderer's hint in the library to stay away.'

'But we really started making progress,' said Pippa, 'when we realised the QWERTY Murderer was not one person, but two working together. Two people, with similar motives but different targets, who agreed to team up in order to achieve them.'

'We checked everyone's alibis for the first two murders,' said Mandy. 'Working on the basis that the murderers basically swapped their targets, it was easy to pick out a group of people with strong alibis for a murder they could benefit from.'

'Then we looked at the scant physical evidence we had,' said Jim Horsley. 'We had two key descriptions. One of a jogger — middle-aged, medium height, dark eyebrows, fairly fit — who had been seen with Sean Davies on the morning of his murder, wearing a loose tracksuit which could easily have concealed a weapon. And one of a woman — a tall, dark, youngish woman wearing bright red lipstick, heavy eyeliner, bright clothes, and a scarf wrapped round her hair. She was loitering in the library at Much Gadding on the same day as a revolving leaflet stand toppled over, requiring fifteen minutes to tidy up. The stand in question was near the door, and we strongly suspect that this woman used the distraction to write a false entry in the borrowers' ledger, claiming that Mrs Parker had borrowed the library copy of *The ABC Murders,* when in fact she had stolen it.'

'And finally,' said Pippa, 'we looked at the employment record, appraisal documents, and prospects of all employees. Of the group we had identified, two stood out. A young reporter, the main wage-earner for her family, who had complained that Janey Dixon was trying to push her out. With the prospect of redundancies, and as the reporter who had the least number of years' service, she would have been likely to go — unless someone else could be removed.'

The crowd began to mutter, and to move away from Jenny Mace.

'The second person worked for the radio station, and had done for many years,' said Mandy. 'The longest-serving DJ apart from Ritz, he always said he deserved the breakfast slot instead of drivetime, and that one day another station would snap him up for their breakfast show. Yet somehow they never did, and his only experience of the breakfast show was filling in for Ritz while he was off sick.'

'You've no right to say these things!' cried Tony Jeffries, stabbing a finger at Mandy. 'What proof do you have? Coming in here accusing innocent people —'

'All right, Tony,' said Inspector Fanshawe. 'We don't go round accusing innocent people. And to make absolutely sure, we devised a couple of, um —'

'Psychological moments,' said Pippa. 'Like in Hercule Poirot.'

'Exactly,' said the inspector. 'The first was when Ritz obligingly choked on his tea a few minutes ago. Most of you looked at Ritz straightaway, either with concern in case he had been poisoned, or exasperation that he was interrupting my exciting narrative. But I observed a panicky exchange of glances between Tony and Jenny, and some subtle head-shaking. Almost as if they were saying to each other: 'Did you do that? I didn't know you were going to do that.'

'I also observed it,' said Jim Horsley. 'And the second psychological moment was when Inspector Fanshawe called Mrs Parker to the front. Again, most of you looked for Mrs Parker, then stared as she came to join us. Our two suspects stared straight ahead, as if they didn't want to betray themselves by being able to identify Mrs Parker by sight. Once they saw where everyone else was looking, they joined in.'

Jenny chewed her lip furiously. 'All right. I admit I was part of it. I didn't kill anyone, though. *He* did all that —'

'That's enough,' said the inspector. 'More than enough.'

Jim and Mandy each pulled out a set of handcuffs and advanced on the crowd, which drew back from Tony and Jenny. Stewart Burgess and Phil grabbed Tony Jeffries by his arms and marched him towards the policeman. 'Take him away, please,' spat Stewart. 'Get him out of here.' And the handcuffs snapped on.

Jenny stood alone, tears streaming down her face. 'Everyone hated her, you know,' she shouted, then rounded on her colleagues. 'You all did, but you just let her go on taking. You'd have let her take my job. No-one ever took my side, and I couldn't stand it any more!' She let Mandy cuff her without resisting.

'Good,' said the inspector. 'We may be calling some of you in to give further evidence' — he eyed Brendan and

Gerald — 'but for now, I strongly suggest you get back to work while we finish up.'

Darren Best unlocked the door and the staff filed out. Some were silent, some murmuring, and some glanced back to Tony and Jenny, standing between the police officers.

'Scaring us like that,' Diane said to Ritz as he got up. She moved to his side and nudged him.

'I was rather good, wasn't I?' said Ritz, grinning.

'At least I'll be able to sleep tonight without worrying I'll be murdered in my bed,' Diane replied, casting an accusing glare at Pippa and the police. She stalked out with her head held high.

'Thank you very much for your help, Mrs Parker,' said Inspector Fanshawe. 'We'll be busy with these two at the station, and I daresay you want to get home to your family.'

Pippa rolled her eyes. 'My husband can manage perfectly well. I just want to get out of this stab vest thing.'

'And that awful outfit,' said Mandy.

Pippa gave her an injured look. 'It isn't my fault if working doesn't suit me.'

Mandy giggled. 'Nice work on the psychological moment,' she said, offering a hand. 'Maybe I should read the books.'

'Maybe,' said Pippa, shaking her hand. 'See you around.' She nodded to Jim Horsley, who tipped his cap to her, and clattered downstairs.

'I knew you were fishy the minute I set eyes on you,' said Diane, as she entered the reception.

Pippa crossed out her alias, wrote *Pippa Parker* in its

place, and added her time of leaving. She looked up to find Diane peering at her. 'What are you, anyway? Some sort of special constable?'

'No,' said Pippa. 'I'm a wife, mother, and PR person. And every so often, I solve murders.' She winked at Diane's bemused face, and went out whistling.

CHAPTER 24

'I now pronounce you husband and wife,' said the registrar. 'You may kiss the bride.'

As Jeff bent to kiss Lila, Pippa let out the breath she had been holding. 'I'm so glad it's over,' she whispered to Simon.

'So am I,' he whispered back. 'You've been like a cat on hot bricks all day.'

The guests applauded, and Lila's sister cheered. Lila's mother, in a hat which resembled a flowery cartwheel, gave her a death-stare which had no effect whatsoever.

'Do you blame me?' whispered Pippa, adjusting the strapless bodice of her dress, which had shifted a little through standing up and sitting down several times in the performance of her duties. 'Bridesmaid *and* wedding organiser. That's way too much responsibility for one day.'

'Well, at least they're married,' said Simon. 'At last.'

'And no-one's wearing a grass skirt,' added Pippa, as Short Back and Sides, led by Lewis, launched into 'I've

Had The Time Of My Life'.

In the end, without murders and fire risk plans to get in the way, the organisation of Lila and Jeff's wedding was so simple that Pippa found herself waking in the night convinced she had forgotten something. Bella, when consulted, had put her foot down very firmly. 'I don't want to wear a silly outfit. I want to wear a pretty dress and you have to wear one too, Mummy. And Jeff has to wear a suit. Not a grass skirt or a . . . *costume.*'

'I feel ridiculous,' Lila had said, when she pulled open the changing-room curtain at Blushes, Gadcester's premier bridal boutique.

'But you look beautiful,' said Pippa. 'And, can I say, slinky.'

'*That's* the dress!' shouted Bella, pointing and beaming, and Lila's sister Jess sniffed loudly. After a couple more glasses of prosecco she confided to Pippa that Jess was short for Jezebel, and she had never forgiven their mother.

Jeff wore a morning suit with a tie that matched Lila's bouquet of red roses. 'I half-expected him to turn up with the quiff,' muttered Simon, when Pippa had taken her seat.

'Don't,' said Pippa. 'I might have had to put that in the fire risk action plan.'

She had been somewhat startled to find Daisy Franks hovering in the hallway when the bridal party had arrived, wearing a plain dark suit and cream blouse. Her blonde quiff was even blonder against her tan. 'Afternoon,' said Daisy, leaning in to shake hands. 'I thought I'd pop down and see how things are going. Don't worry, your registrar's here and everything's in order.'

'Thank you for approving the venue,' said Lila. 'I don't know what we'd have done otherwise.'

'Got hitched somewhere else, I expect,' said Daisy, and winked. 'It looks brill.'

The Hall did, indeed, look brill. Though chilly, there was a pale blue sky and a weak sun lighting the pale stone. The lawns were immaculate, Dot the florist had supplied a wreath for the door to match Lila's bouquet, and Serendipity had hand-lettered a sign: *Lila and Jeff's Wedding: This Way.* Inside, the staircase was dressed with ribbons.

Lila's father was waiting outside the dining-room door for them. 'Took your time,' he said, and winked.

Lila gasped at the room, dressed with roses and ribbons, and the guests oohed and aahed at Bella and her cousin Mia, scattering rose petals in their pretty dresses, and then at Lila in her white column gown. As Pippa moved up the aisle she could see Jeff in the front row, wiping away a tear. *This is going to be a cracker,* she thought.

But nevertheless, she was glad it was over. She accepted a glass of Buck's Fizz from Beryl and drank half of it in one go.

'Steady,' warned Simon. 'You don't want to look tiddly in the photos.'

'Wedding organisation is thirsty work,' said Pippa. 'Ruby, would you like a drink?'

Ruby, in Simon's arms, rubbed her eyes and stretched her hand towards Pippa's glass.

'Maybe not this drink,' said Pippa. 'Freddie, come with

me and we'll get something for you too.'

'When can I take this off?' asked Freddie, plucking at his shirt collar.

Pippa bent down, carefully, and undid the top button of his shirt. 'Is that better?' Freddie gasped for air like a goldfish, and she laughed. 'You're worse than Ruby!'

'Bridesmaids, best man, flower girls and ushers, please!' called the photographer. He had been recommended by Gerald Tamblyn, who was lurking near the drinks table, notebook in hand, to cover 'the first wedding at Higginbotham Hall', as he had put it on the phone. Pippa suspected the prospect of free drinks and content for the paper had motivated his generous offer, but she wasn't about to turn it down. She sighed, found two glasses of squash, and delivered them with Freddie to Simon, before adjusting her bodice yet again and heading off to pose on the staircase.

'Let's get the kids to Mum's after this,' said Simon, out of the side of his mouth, as the wedding party posed for one last photo on the steps of the Hall. 'They're both exhausted.'

'That's what comes of bouncing on their beds at five in the morning from excitement,' Pippa murmured back. 'If it wasn't for under-eye concealer Lila would be wondering how a panda gatecrashed her wedding.'

'You look lovely to me,' said Simon, and sneaked a quick kiss, which of course was one of the photos to appear in the *Gadcester Chronicle* the following Monday.

***

'Ding ding, round two,' said Simon, as they walked up

213

the gravel drive hand in hand.

Pippa had taken the opportunity of a nap between dropping the children off and getting ready for the reception. Even so, she wasn't sure she'd last beyond nine thirty. 'I honestly don't know how we used to party until two,' she said.

'It's the kids, they drain your life force like vampires,' said Simon.

'True.' Pippa sighed. 'I don't know how Miss Darcy copes with thirty of them all day.'

'Maybe she's a vampire,' Simon replied.

Pippa snorted. 'If she is, Declan doesn't seem to mind.'

The talking-things-over-with-Declan supper was somewhat complicated by his arrival with an additional guest: Miss Darcy, dressed to party rather than dinner party. 'You don't mind, do you?' he asked Simon. 'I completely forgot I was meant to go clubbing in Gadcester with Jade tonight.'

'Um, no,' said Simon. 'That's fine.'

Pippa was tempted to say 'Hello, Miss Darcy,' but somehow it didn't seem quite fitting. Miss Darcy's eyes had opened very wide when she saw Pippa, but otherwise she had not acknowledged their prior acquaintance.

They had managed to stretch the chicken to four, after which Simon had attempted to engage Declan in merger conversation, while Miss Darcy (as Pippa couldn't help calling her in her head) fidgeted beside him on the sofa. They had left at ten o'clock, and Pippa had a sneaking suspicion that Miss Darcy would get Declan to a nightclub if she had to drag him there herself.

'She's Freddie's teacher,' she said, as Simon closed the door.

Simon goggled at her. 'You're kidding.'

'I think Miss Darcy maintains a strict work-life balance,' said Pippa. 'But if she ever mentions Freddie's reading record again I shall think of her in that little silver dress, glued to poor Declan, and smile.'

She smiled now, thinking of it. 'Did you ever talk things through with Declan?'

'Nah,' said Simon. 'His mind's, um, somewhere else. We'll work things out, don't worry. And we can't waste valuable couple time talking about work.'

Lady Higginbotham opened the door, dressed in her smartest cashmere jumper. 'Oh good, Pippa. Would you two mind helping Serendipity with the cake?'

Beryl was hovering, and Pippa could hear the *thump-thump-thump* of a lively wedding disco. 'I'd do it myself,' Beryl said, 'but I'm worried I'll wobble.'

'I never even thought about cake insurance,' said Lady Higginbotham.

'Does that exist?' asked Simon.

'It certainly ought to,' she said, grimly.

'It just needs lifting out, and it's already on a board,' said Serendipity. 'But it is a two-person job.' She beckoned Pippa closer, and whispered 'And everyone else is too chicken. I'd have brought it earlier, but Lady Higginbotham insisted I wait until half an hour before it's due to be cut.'

Pippa rolled her eyes. 'Come on, let's do this. Simon, if we lift the cake can you shift the box out from under it?'

She peered into the box. 'Oh, Serendipity, it's gorgeous.'

'Ready?' asked Serendipity, reaching into the box.

'Ready,' said Pippa, grasping the edge of the board and hoping that she was.

'Slow and steady . . . one, two, three, lift!'

'Box is clear,' called Simon. 'Repeat, box is clear.'

'And down,' said Serendipity. 'Phew.'

'Wow.' The bottom tier was deep red, the middle tier white and painted with red roses, and the top tier was pure white, with icing flowers and a miniature Lila, Jeff and Bella on the top.

'Fruit cake, red velvet cake, vanilla sponge,' said Serendipity. 'And the red matches your dress, how about that?'

'It must have taken you hours,' said Pippa.

'It took my mind off other things,' said Serendipity. 'Plus I'm baking one rather like it for the show pilot.' She smiled shyly. 'Ashley thinks it'll really take off.'

'I'll go and get drinks,' said Simon. 'Wine, Pip?'

'Please,' Pippa said, still gazing at the cake. 'I'll join you in a minute.'

'Just follow the sound of banging,' said Beryl, heading for the kitchen.

Pippa touched Serendipity's arm. 'I'm glad it worked out.'

'So am I,' said Serendipity. 'And that I rang Mummy.'

'Is their show going ahead?' asked Pippa.

'She doesn't know,' replied Serendipity. 'But she's glad we're speaking again.' She eyed Pippa. 'Did your friend Suze ever...'

'Apologise? No.' Pippa sighed. 'I think she's licking her wounds. Maybe we'll talk, eventually. But now, let's go and dance.'

***

'Let's hear some NOISE!' bellowed Ritz Robertson as they entered the Long Room, and the cheers from the dance floor completely drowned out 'Hi Ho Silver Lining.'

'Pippa!' Lila weaved through the dancers. She was still in her wedding dress, now teamed with a pair of Converse high-tops. 'Where've you been? Why aren't you dancing?'

'I've been sorting out your cake!'

'Fabulous,' said Jeff, appearing from nowhere and leading Lila back to the dance floor.

Pippa scanned the room, trying to pick out the people she knew from the tight groups of 'people from work'. There was Imogen, leaning down to dance with Henry. Eva was slow-dancing with her husband, while Caitlin was sitting with Sam at the edge of the dance floor, cradling Josh on her lap and tapping her foot. Jess was whispering in the ear of Jeff's brother Frankie, and giggling. Lila's and Jeff's parents were sitting together at a round table to the side, watching too. And Lila and Jeff themselves were dancing so close that you couldn't have fitted a pin between them.

Simon emerged from the throng with a glass of wine and a pint. 'Here you go,' he said. 'I didn't know if you wanted red or white, so I got pink.'

'Lovely.' She took a sip, ignoring Lila's frenzied beckoning.

He took a long pull on his pint, then put an arm round

her waist. 'All OK?'

'Yes.' She sighed with relief. 'Marrying done, buffet's here, Ritz is doing his job, the cake's in one piece and Sheila has the kids.'

'And murders solved. For now.'

She raised her eyebrows. 'Why are you bringing that up?'

Simon shrugged. 'It just came to mind. I mean, you said you'd retired before, and then look what happened.'

'I won't make that mistake again.'

'I suppose you can never say never.'

'True.'

Simon put down his drink and steered Pippa to the dance floor. 'The night is young. Let's get a dance or two in before Lila's glass slippers turn into — oh, they already did.'

Pippa giggled in spite of herself and drained her glass.

'One for the romantics!' called Ritz. '"Lady in Red", come on you know you want to!'

Pippa groaned. 'No you don't,' said Simon, and put his arms around her. 'You're wearing red, you *have* to. It's the law.'

'Aww,' said Lila, as they swayed past each other. 'Look at you two.'

Look at us, indeed, thought Pippa, as Simon sang along in her ear. *We made it.* In spite of murders and crises and double-crossing and an attempt on my life, we're still standing. And that's worth a lot. Even if I do have to put up with his singing. And as they spun slowly round the dance floor, she decided that she wouldn't have it any other way.

218

BONUS MATERIAL - RECIPES A LA PIPPA

Spaghetti Parkernaise

1.   Turn the fridge out hunting for the minced beef, then remember that you put it in the freezer because the last time you put it in the fridge with good intentions, you forgot about it.

2.   Retrieve solid block of mince from freezer. Mmm. Get mild frostbite while removing mince from packet. Look for microwave manual. How long *does* it take to defrost mince?

3.   Microwave manual not in kitchen drawer. Or dining-room drawer. Peer at model number and find manual on the internet. We're getting somewhere!

4.   Great. Mince revolving. Banish thoughts of food poisoning from improperly-defrosted mince. But why is there only one tin of chopped tomatoes? And the last onion

left is the smallest one in the world. Plus the garlic has a green shoot growing out of the top. Is that normal?

5.   Look at clock. Surely it can't be half six already.

6.   Check on kids, who are fighting over the blue cushion. Whyyyyyyyy?

7.   *Ping!* As if on cue, Simon walks in. 'Is dinner ready? I'm starving.'

8.   Bite back snarky comment. Pull packet of spaghetti and jar of ready-made sauce out of the cupboard. 'Not too long now.'

9.   Add chopped tomatoes, onions, mushrooms, basil plant and garlic to the shopping list. Getting one's five a day is very important.

10.   Serve spag bog. Wish you'd remembered to get Freddie to change out of his white T-shirt first.

Freddie's MegaMoose cupcakes

1. Assemble cupcake ingredients. I mean, how hard can it be? Flour, baking powder, cocoa powder, eggs, sugar, cupcake cases. And specially-bought Matchmakers for the antlers.

2. Normal sugar, yes. Caster sugar, yes. But where's the icing sugar? Get everything out of the cupboard and find a two-thirds empty packet at the back. That'll be enough. Won't it?

3. Why don't the cupcake cases fit the tin?

4. Whizz up mix. That actually looks all right. And it tastes nice too. Definitely deserves a celebratory Matchmaker.

5. Preheat oven and get cakes in.

6. Find food colouring for icing. Red, yes. Blue, yes. Yellow, yes. Brown, no.

7. If this wasn't meant to be a surprise you could ask Freddie how to mix colours to make brown. Gah. Google 'how to make brown'. Oh OK. You should have known that really.

8. Why does icing sugar turn to almost nothing when you add water? Whyyyyyyyyyyy?

9. Add food colouring, very carefully, and mix. That colour is horrible but no more icing sugar left.

10. Timer goes off. Cupcakes have spread out rather than rising. They look like discuses.

11. Ice discuses with yucky brown icing. Add white choc buttons and a spot of brown icing for eyes. Raisins for nose and mouth.

12. You fool, Pippa, antlers have branches. Briefly consider getting twigs from garden as substitutes. Icing not strong enough to glue branches onto the main Matchmaker.

13. Serve. You wouldn't eat one but Freddie seems to appreciate the effort. Even though he says MegaMoose has blue eyes.

Ruby's rainbow cake

1.   Yes this is ambitious, but you have Serendipity's recipe from her book and she says it never fails. And you've borrowed her cake tins, and bought *everything* in advance.

2.   Mix sponge. See. Dead easy.

3.   Divide by 7. Ah. Should have weighed the mixing bowl first.

4.   Hmm. Make a cuppa while pondering.

5.   OK. Weigh a slightly larger bowl and a slightly smaller bowl and work out the average on phone.

6.   That'll do.

7.   Spend next ten minutes assembling all clean bowls in the house (this involves emptying the fruit bowl). Weigh each and write result in notebook. Then transfer spoonfuls of mixture between the bowls until reasonably sure each has same weight of mixture in it. This takes another half hour.

8.   There's more in that bowl on the right. Reach for tea while contemplating bowl and also that experiment in primary school where the same amount of water looks different in differently-shaped containers. The tea is cold.

9.   Now for the colours. After the MegaMoose cupcake incident, you have bought each shade. See, you learnt something.

10.   Although that green was a lot nicer in the bottle. Maybe it'll look nice once the sponge is baked.

11.   First two sponges IN. And the level of mix looks exactly the same! Result!

12. *Ping!*

13. Why is one sponge twice as big as the other? Don't worry, you can trim it.

14. Next two. When these come out one has sunk in the middle and the other one has risen more on one side.

15. All sponges out. Stack them on top of each other to judge effect. Make a strong cup of tea and find a sharp knife. For the cake. Not Serendipity.

16. First sponge to be trimmed bends alarmingly. Put it down quick. Drink tea. Consider wine. Make cream cheese icing.

17. Who thought anyone would want food coloured snot-green?

18. Cake is sandwiched together. It looks as if it's had too much wine.

19. Hide evidence of baking ineptitude with lots of cream cheese icing.

20. Study finished cake. Can you really serve that at your daughter's birthday? Will she cry? Or will it become a family legend? That time Mummy made a cake with snot in the middle?

21. Phone Serendipity and beg a special favour. Open wine. Job done!

ACKNOWLEDGEMENTS

First of all, thank you to my wonderful and super-speedy beta readers: Carol Bissett, Ruth Cunliffe, Paula Harmon, and Stephen Lenhardt.

And an equally big thank you to John Croall, who proofread the book for me. I checked the murders with him in advance this time — talk about organisation!

I would also like to thank Gareth Dunning, deputy editor of the *Warrington Guardian*, who very kindly allowed me to ask him heaps of questions about how a newspaper is run. I'd like to stress that when I visited all the staff seemed very nice and not at all murderous.

I chomped my way through stacks of Agatha Christie books as a teenager and I still read them now. *The ABC Murders* is one of my favourites, and inspired this book. If you haven't read *The ABC Murders*, you're in for a treat — and I really hope I haven't given too much of the story away.

As always, my husband Stephen Lenhardt gets a thank-you all to himself for his support. I bend his ear about the struggles and tribulations I have with each book, and then, to add insult to injury, I make him read it!

And my last thank you is to you, the reader. I hope you've enjoyed reading Pippa's latest case, and if you could leave a review for the book on Amazon or Goodreads I'd appreciate it very much. Reviews, however short, help other readers to discover books.

FONT AND IMAGE CREDITS

Fonts:

MURDER font: Edo Regular by Vic Fieger (freeware): www.fontsquirrel.com/fonts/Edo

QWERTY font: Type Keys by Typadelic (freeware): www.fontspace.com/typadelic/type-keys

Classic font: Nimbus Roman No9 L by URW++: www.fontsquirrel.com/fonts/nimbus-roman-no9-l. License — GNU General Public License v2.00: www.fontsquirrel.com/license/nimbus-roman-no9-l

Script font: Dancing Script OT by Impallari Type: www.fontsquirrel.com/fonts/dancing-script-ot. License – SIL Open Font License v.1.10: http://scripts.sil.org/OFL

Graphics:

Hall taken from Medieval ancient castles vector created by macrovector: https://www.freepik.com/free-vector/

ABOUT THE AUTHOR

Liz Hedgecock grew up in London, England, did an English degree, and then took forever to start writing. After several years working in the National Health Service, some short stories crept into the world. A few even won prizes. Then the stories started to grow longer...

Now Liz travels between the nineteenth and twenty-first centuries, murdering people. To be fair, she does usually clean up after herself.

Liz's reimaginings of Sherlock Holmes, her Pippa Parker cozy mystery series, and the Caster & Fleet Victorian mystery series (written with Paula Harmon), are available in ebook and paperback.

Liz lives in Cheshire with her husband and two sons, and when she's not writing or child-wrangling you can usually find her reading, messing about on Twitter, or cooing over stuff in museums and art galleries. That's her story, anyway, and she's sticking to it.

Website/blog: http://lizhedgecock.wordpress.com
Facebook: http://www.facebook.com/lizhedgecockwrites
Twitter: http://twitter.com/lizhedgecock
Goodreads: https://www.goodreads.com/lizhedgecock

BOOKS BY LIZ HEDGECOCK

Short stories
The Secret Notebook of Sherlock Holmes
Bitesize
The Adventure of the Scarlet Rosebud

Halloween Sherlock series (novelettes)
The Case of the Snow-White Lady
Sherlock Holmes and the Deathly Fog
The Case of the Curious Cabinet

Sherlock & Jack series (novellas)
A Jar Of Thursday
Something Blue
A Phoenix Rises

Mrs Hudson & Sherlock Holmes series (novels)
A House Of Mirrors
In Sherlock's Shadow

Pippa Parker Mysteries (novels)
Murder At The Playgroup
Murder In The Choir
A Fete Worse Than Death
Murder in the Meadow

The QWERTY Murders

Caster & Fleet Mysteries (with Paula Harmon)
The Case of the Black Tulips
The Case of the Runaway Client
The Case of the Deceased Clerk
The Case of the Masquerade Mob
The Case of the Fateful Legacy
The Case of the Crystal Kisses

For children (with Zoe Harmon)
A Christmas Carrot

WHITE
RHINO
BOOKS